NORTH BY NORTHANGER

Rebecca H. Jamison

Library of Congress Control Number: 9781696043663

Cover design by Shaela Kay Odd

CHAPTER 1

I thought I was going on my first ever blind date. Instead, I got kidnapped.

It all started with a phone call from my big brother, Wade, who was going to school a few hours away in Houston. "How would you like to come up here this weekend? I've got a roommate, Clayton, I think you'd like to meet. Doesn't the Angelina College spring break start on Friday? We could meet for lunch."

"Yeah, our spring break starts Friday, but I don't know about a date," I said. I'd heard my friends' bad-blind-date stories, and I wasn't sure I could trust Wade's matchmaking skills.

"We're going to an escape room, you know, one of those places where you have to solve a mystery and—"

"—I know what an escape room is." He thought because he'd finally moved to the big city that he knew so much more than I did.

"It's got a Hitchcock theme," he added, drawing out his vowels.

He had me there. I'd been obsessed with Hitchcock movies—any sort of mystery movies actually—since third grade. Now, though I'd graduated from high school two years earlier and was going to the community college near our home, I still managed to keep up with my hobby. If I had to endure a blind date in order to visit a Hitchcock-themed escape room, so be it. "I'm in," I said.

He told me that he was dating Clayton's sister. Then he went on describing Clayton, and it sounded as if his new girlfriend had written out a list of notes about her brother—how smart he was, how he was pre-med and had his own car. Blah, blah, blah. Then, right before Wade had to get to class, he added. "There's just one thing—"

"What?"

"No vintage clothes."

I raised my voice much more than I should have on the phone. "You know I always wear vintage."

We have a big family. I won't say how big because every time I say the number, something shuts off inside people. Their mouths hang open and their eyes blink. Then, as if that wasn't bad enough, they either make a joke about my parents' sex life or they lie about how nice it must be to have so many siblings.

Alright. I'll say it. My parents have ten children. Five sons. Five daughters. I'm number six—right smack in the middle, so it was either hand-me-downs or thrift store fashion. That's how I picked up my penchant for wearing vintage clothing. My clothes were the best way I could find to stand out.

"Can't you make an exception just this once?" Wade asked. He should have known better.

"I'll think about it."

I could hear him exhale. "Okay. I'll see you Friday at noon. I've gotta get to class."

When Friday came, I was seriously tempted to wear a neon T-shirt and holographic pants to meet this Clayton guy. If we hadn't been going to that Hitchcock escape room, I probably would have, but this occasion called for a little more elegance— fifties elegance. After slipping into my sky blue taffeta dress, I pulled my hair up in a simple chignon, slapped on some pearls, slipped my phone into my red clutch purse, and wore my white patent-leather pumps. Yes, the white gloves were probably a bit much, especially since I was driving Dad's old pickup, but there's nothing like white gloves to complete a look.

The place where we'd agreed to meet was better than I expected. It was an old-style diner with shiny chrome accents. A long counter ran beside the kitchen, and a row of booths sat beneath the large windows. The floorplan was straight out of the fifties. Wade must have really wanted me to like this roommate of his.

Since I was twenty minutes early, I sat down at the counter and ordered myself a red cream soda while I got out my phone to text Wade. I was enjoying my first sip of soda, when in walked the perfect leading man—if this had been a movie. He was tall with wide shoulders, and his dark hair swept across his forehead with the slightest wave. He wore a light blue button-up shirt untucked over jeans.

Though every single stool at the bar was available, he sat two seats down from me—with just one seat between us. Now that I think about it, that should have been a warning. Handsome men didn't ever choose to sit near me. I never quite understood why that was—perhaps the Morland family's conservative reputation or a distrust of girls who wore vintage clothing.

Without bothering to think, I closed the gap between us by sliding myself, my phone, and my drink toward him.

He smiled and looked like he was about to say something, but the server approached. "Hi Grant," she said. "What can I get you?"

The name Grant suited him—a little Cary, a little Hugh. He seemed like the type who could fit in at the governor's mansion as well as a monster truck rally.

He ordered an orange juice—nothing more. After the server left, he studied me a moment, taking in my dress, my gloves, my pale pink lipstick. "Let me guess. Pretty blond hair, white gloves, a fifties-style dress. You're channeling Princess Grace of Monaco."

"Close," I said. "I'm channeling Grace Kelly. You know, the actress."

He squinted his eyes, as if he thought I might be trying to trick him. Then he laughed. "Grace Kelly. I should have known. Are you going to a costume party later?"

"No. I'm here to meet my brother. He's setting me up with his roommate." I couldn't help making a face when I said roommate.

He leaned toward me and groaned. "A blind date. Brutal."

"I only agreed because we're going to an escape room, and I've been dying to go to one. Have you ever been?"

He lifted one eyebrow. "No, but it's on my bucket list." The corner of his lip twitched, letting me know he wasn't really the type to keep a bucket list.

"You should come with us." The words came out as soon as I thought them, but I didn't regret the invitation at all.

7

For a second, he struggled to hide his smile, but it broke through. "I'm sure your brother wouldn't appreciate you bringing a plus one to your blind date."

He had a point. Wade wouldn't be pleased. Then again, once Wade saw my blue taffeta dress, he'd be upset with me anyway.

The server brought the orange juice, but Grant kept his gaze on me. "It's probably better if you just tell them about the mysterious stranger you met at the diner. Say something like, 'he looked at me with hungry eyes.'"

I was drinking my soda when he said this, and had a bit of a laughing-choking fit before I could respond. "Kind of like the wolf in 'Little Red Riding Hood'?"

He leaned toward me, baring his teeth, which were, I must admit, much too straight and white to conjure up images of a wolf. "Exactly like that."

I laughed, placing my elbow on the counter and propping my chin up. "What else shall I say?"

"That you enjoyed the mysterious stranger's playful banter and that you wished you could have spent the evening with him instead of with—what is the name of the roommate?"

"Clayton."

He shook his head. "Instead of with Clayton." His pitch dove down at least an octave at the end of Clayton's name, making it sound oh so dull.

Flirting with Grant came so easily, I barely had to think before I knew my next response. "The problem with your story is that you're not a mysterious stranger. I already know your name is Grant and that you probably either live or work around here."

For a split second, his forehead crinkled and he dropped his gaze. Then his expression relaxed and he took a swig of orange juice. "You're quite the detective."

"The server said your name," I explained, "which means you're a regular. That's why I said you live or work nearby, unless you come here to visit your grandmother."

"Do I seem like the type to visit my grandmother every week?"

That meant he was here every week. "Most definitely, and just so we're even, my name is Eva." I held my hand out to him. "Was I right? Do you work around here?"

I expected he would tell me a little more about himself then. Instead, he asked where I was from, and I ended up spilling half my life story—how I was majoring in forensic science at the community college, how our small country town only had 965 residents, how I liked to watch old episodes of the Monk TV show, and how I shared a bedroom with my younger sister.

I was just about to tell him about our pet love birds when I realized I was talking way too much. "What is it you do for a living?" I asked. "Or are you in school too?"

"I work for the family business," he said, and right as I was about to ask what kind of business his family ran, his phone buzzed. He took out his phone, which happened to be the same exact model as mine, and just like mine, it didn't have a case.

"Oops," he said, reading through the text. "I've got to get going." He put his phone down on the counter, gulped down his orange juice and slapped down a five-dollar bill. "It was nice to meet you, Eva."

I sat there like a new kid in seventh grade, shocked that this life-changing moment was coming to such a screeching halt. "Nice to meet you too." He wasn't about to walk out of the restaurant without even asking for my number, was he?

He was indeed. Before I knew what was happening, the heavy glass door was swinging shut behind him, letting out an electronic bell tone.

I was once again alone with my cream soda.

This was the closest I'd ever come to love at first sight. I mean, Grant and I—we just clicked. He knew about Grace Kelly and he made me laugh. It was like I'd been living with only one side of a zipper my whole entire life, and now, zztt, I'd found the other side and I was complete—an entire evening gown. Until he left.

I picked up my phone, deciding to console myself with a little internet surfing, but when I swiped the screen, it prompted me for a password. My phone didn't require a password. Grant had taken my phone instead of his.

I had a good ten minutes before Wade was due to arrive, which meant I had at least fifteen minutes to chase Grant down. (Wade was always late.) "I'll be back in a second," I told the server as I rushed to the door. "Grant took my phone instead of his."

But she bolted ahead of me, holding out my check as she stood beside the door. "He'll be back for it. He forgets his phone all the time. I'll be your cashier."

"I think I'd better go find him. It might take him a while to realize he has my phone instead of his," I said, fumbling to get my wallet out of my red clutch purse. As I sorted through the bills, I remembered seeing movies where detectives exchanged cash for information. I flipped open my wallet and handed her four dollars, which would provide her with a one-dollar-and-fifty-four-cent tip. "Keep the change."

She looked like she could barely refrain from rolling her eyes.

I pushed open the door to look up and down the street. Shielding my eyes from the midafternoon sun, I saw no sign of Grant in the parking lot or in the street. I handed her another dollar. "Here, keep this too. Do you happen to know where Grant might have gone? He said he works for his family. Do you know his last name?"

She crinkled her nose, making me think she might not tell me even if she did know. "I think his last name's Tilney, but I could be wrong. All I know about his job is that he drives a truck, and he works around the corner."

"Thanks." I took off running out the door, my skirt flapping around me as I ran across the parking lot in my kitten heels. Grant Tilney. Such a noble name. Maybe his company had his name in it—Tilney Enterprises, Tilney Corporation, Tilney Towers.

Coming to the intersection of two streets, I stood on tiptoes, looking down one street, then the next. This area of town was what I would describe as a warehouse district with lots of eighteen-wheelers coming up and down the streets but very little traffic otherwise. A few of the buildings had signs out front, but nothing with the name Tilney on it. The server had said he worked just around the corner, but which corner? And how far away was just around the corner?

Another problem was that I hadn't bothered to notice whether Grant had come to the restaurant on foot or in a vehicle. Nor did I know what kind of car or truck he drove. But I couldn't give up.

I hopped in my pickup. Looking around, it seemed the most likely direction for a trucker to work was toward the right, so I turned right, and drove until I came to the first warehouse that had trucks parked beside it. There was no sign on the gray building, just the address 288 B. The server had said Grant worked just around the corner. This had to be it.

I parked and walked up to the plain metal door painted white. A sign beside the door read "Ring for service."

I rang.

Then I began to feel silly. What kind of woman, after all, rings a random doorbell on the side of a warehouse to return the phone of a guy that she just barely met? I could have just as easily called my phone from the diner. Then he would have tried to answer it and realized it wasn't his. But I had already rung the doorbell, and I could hear footsteps on the other side of the door. It was too late to turn back now.

The door swung open and a tall, dark-haired man greeted me. "May I help you?" He spoke with a foreign accent—perhaps Middle Eastern.

"Yes," I stammered. "I'm looking for a man named Grant Tilney. We accidentally exchanged phones at the diner. Does he work here?"

His face remained passive. I couldn't tell whether he knew Grant or not. "Come inside."

I stepped inside the dimly lit warehouse that held rows of industrial-size shelves stacked twenty feet high with boxes. The man led me to a wall along the side of the warehouse, where he opened a door. "You may wait here," he said.

I walked into the small office, which looked like it belonged in a fancy office building, complete with plush chairs, a mahogany desk, an oriental rug, and a large oil painting of Venice.

Now that I was standing still, I wondered once again if I should have just waited at the diner for Grant to come back. He was probably there right now, listening to the server explain about the crazy girl who almost didn't pay for her drink. This was just like me to act without thinking things through.

Still, this had to be where Grant worked. Why else would the man have invited me inside? He shut the door behind him, and I was left by myself, standing in front of the giant desk, looking for some clue as to whether it belonged to Grant.

Just my luck, the desk was mostly bare. Except for a cup full of pens and a notepad, there was nothing to identify the person who worked there. The bookshelf on the other side of the room held only a large Chinese vase and a television. I couldn't find a single brochure or business card. All I could find were a few words scrawled on the notepad: "Find Leslie Kaplan."

I'd known a girl named Leslie at school, but I'd never met anyone named Kaplan. Still, it sounded familiar. Had I heard it in a movie?

The minutes ticked away, and as they did, I felt stupider and stupider. Grant was going to think I was desperate—tracking him down at his work. The server had said he left his phone all the time. He'd probably already realized what had happened and gone back to exchange phones. The normal thing would have been for me to wait for him at the diner.

I opened the door and peeked out. Nothing.

Then I heard footsteps approaching. He was coming after all. I shut the door, pasted on a smile, and sat in the chair, hoping Grant wouldn't think I was too desperate to track him down like this.

But when the door opened, it wasn't Grant. It was the man who'd invited me inside. "She's in here, Ingrid," he said.

A severe-looking middle-aged woman walked in. She was about medium height with gray hair cut into a straight bob. She wore a black suit. "Hello," she said, not bothering to extend her hand. She didn't make eye contact but spoke quickly, as if she wanted to get this whole thing over and done with. "Can I get your name?" Like the man, she had an accent, and I guessed she'd been sent to get rid of me.

"I was just wondering if Grant Tilney works here. You see we have the same phone, and after we met at the diner, he accidentally took mine instead of his." I kept the phone against my chest. Surely, if Grant were here, he'd come apologize for exchanging phones with me.

"First, I'd like to know your name," she said.

The last thing I needed was for her to tell Grant about the silly girl named Eva who tracked him down to his work. On the other hand, if he didn't work here, why would she need to know my name? So instead of giving my own name, I said the first name that came to mind. "I'm Leslie Kaplan," I said, "and if you can't answer my question, I'm leaving."

The expression on her face went from stormy to sunny in an instant. "Leslie Kaplan. Oh, well this is a good day after all." I made my way to the door, but she moved faster, placing her hand on the door knob. "Come this way," she said to me as she opened the door. Then she turned to the man who'd let me inside the warehouse. "You know what to do, Ronald."

I was hoping this meant I was finally going to get to see Grant. Then I caught sight of Ronald, and I froze. It was like in a movie where someone has a gun in his pocket and points it at someone else. Was that object in his coat pocket a gun? "Come on," Ingrid ordered, yanking me by the elbow. "We're going this way."

I wanted to scream, but no sound came out. I dropped Grant's phone to the floor.

Wait! Things like this didn't happen to me. This couldn't be real. That was just the sort of thing Wade would do to trick me. One Halloween, he'd convinced me to go to the cemetery with him, where his friends were all dressed up as ghosts and hiding behind the monuments.

13

"Did my brother put you guys up to this?" I asked Ingrid. "Is he playing a trick on me?" That had to be what was going on. He had decided to create a different kind of escape room.

Ingrid didn't respond, and I studied her face, trying to figure out if she was acting a part. Her eyes stared forward in the direction she was pulling me, out into the empty warehouse with its rows of enormous shelves. Maybe this was real. Had I gotten involved in a mob war? Did Leslie Kaplan have a price on her head? Were there drugs in some of these boxes?

I swallowed, willing my voice back into existence. "I'm not really Leslie Kaplan," I said, my voice trembling. "I just saw her name on the notepad in the office. I can show you my I.D. if you want."

Ronald and Ingrid turned to each other, sending a silent message through nods and eye movements.

I hadn't been so scared since the first day of kindergarten, and just like on that day, I was in danger of peeing my pants.

But I had to hold myself together. I grasped the red clutch purse. The door was about ten yards away, and my pickup a few steps beyond that. I lunged, breaking free from Ingrid's grasp and running toward the door, but just as I touched the doorknob, Ronald slammed against me, pushing me against the wall. It was way too much force for this to be one of my brother's role-playing games.

"I swear I'm not Leslie Kaplan," I cried as he twisted my arm behind my back. I still held my purse in my other hand. "You can check my license. My name's Eva Morland." If I could just get out of the warehouse—even if I had to leave my purse behind. I held it out to Ronald.

He was about to take it when Ingrid cackled a high-pitched, nasal laugh and snatched my purse from my hands, sending it scuttling across the concrete floor. "Don't be an idiot, Ronald."

"Grant!" I screamed. "Help me!" But my voice simply echoed off the surrounding walls. Wherever I was, it wasn't Grant's place of employment.

The entire time I'd been here, I'd only seen Ronald and Ingrid. I hadn't heard the purr of machinery or the echo of

14

another's footsteps. It was likely these two were the only ones in this place.

With Ingrid walking behind us, Ronald pulled me to the other side of the warehouse as I fought with all my might to break free. He was stronger, though, and my shoes had no traction on the smooth, cement floor. A black sedan was parked just outside. Ingrid opened its door. "Get inside," she ordered as I wrestled against Ronald

Remembering all the stories I'd heard of kidnappings, I knew this wouldn't end well. I stomped on Ronald's foot with my heel, twisting free from his grasp.

He pulled the gun from his pocket, pointing it straight at me. "Get in the car or I'll shoot." His hands were trembling.

Ingrid seemed less nervous. She dug her nails into my arm, but I kicked her, and she fell back.

"Someone help me!" I screamed.

"Push her in," Ingrid ordered. Then both Ronald and Ingrid rushed me, bumping my head as they pushed me into the sedan. I wasn't going easily, though. When they tried to slam the door shut, I kicked it back open with both feet.

Then a deafening thud shook the car. My ears ringing, I looked up to see a bullet hole in the car's upholstery, just an inch from my shoulder. "Cooperate, or I shoot," Ronald hissed.

I decided being kidnapped wasn't as bad as being dead.

Chapter 2

With Ronald in the driver's seat and Ingrid beside me, I inched my hand toward the door handle. Sure, I was having the most sophisticated drive of my life with new car smell wafting around me and cupholders all over the place, as well as a sun roof. But the door handle wouldn't budge when I unlocked it and pulled—they'd probably flipped the child lock switch on the side of the door—and the tinted windows made it so that no one could see me from outside when I signaled for help.

I was hoping the condition of the car meant they wouldn't want to kill me inside it and mess up all the nice carpet and leather. Even so, I took off my white gloves and removed my heels, preparing to fight back when the time came.

As we reached the suburbs of Houston, Ingrid spoke into her phone. "We found Leslie Kaplan. I've got her in the car with me. Do you want me to bring her to the ranch?"

I shivered at the word ranch. It sounded isolated enough for a murder.

I couldn't make out what the person on the other end said.

"Her purse is on the floor at P2," Ingrid responded. "I didn't have time to search it … Yes, ma'am. We'll take care of it."

If I had my phone, I could have looked up Leslie Kaplan and figured out what this kidnapping was all about. Her name sounded American enough, but I'd never heard of her, so this probably wasn't a high-profile kidnapping that would involve ransoms—unless she had a lot of money.

We drove for an hour and a half according to the clock on the car when Ronald spoke up. "I haven't eaten lunch yet. We'll have to stop at a drive-through. Do you fancy a Big Mac?"

"What do you think this is?" Ingrid shot back. "A day trip? If we stop, she might get away."

Ronald took a moment to respond. "There's a McDonald's in three miles."

Ingrid heaved a sigh. "We're not stopping."

16

Ronald huffed. "We're not stopping," he mimicked in a high-pitched voice. "And you ask me why Marco blocked your phone number."

I giggled. I couldn't help it. I get that way when I'm scared.

Ingrid whipped her head around, glaring at me. "Enough from you," she snarled.

They grew quiet again, and I watched the road signs, memorizing the route we followed. I was also mouthing the word "help" to passengers in other cars on the off chance that the sun would hit the tinted window in just the right way for people to see me. Only one man seemed to notice, but he turned away, probably thinking that I was playing some sort of prank.

This wasn't good. I gulped. Feeling myself starting to hyperventilate, I gazed down at my blue taffeta dress. It had helped me cope in so many other situations—my job interview at the town hall, my date with Beau Whitaker, my speech class final, my vlogging debut.

This, though, this demanded more coping than I'd ever had to muster. All I could do was pray.

Part of me was terrified that I was going to be chopped up and buried in a hole on some remote ranch while ten mangy-looking crows stood guard.

But another part of me wanted to daydream about what might happen after my painful death. The news media would have a heyday speculating about my fate. My siblings would hold Eva searches all around Houston. Best of all, my vlogs would finally become popular. I could get up to 10,000 shares on my "Comeback of Clip-On Earrings" video.

Then, if my vlogs went viral, fashion designers might name a line after me—the Eva Morland collection of fifties-style dresses, purses, and gloves. Everyone would be walking around in swing skirts and cinched waists. I'd actually be doing society a favor by dying—bringing a sense of style to a T-shirt-wearing nation.

On the other hand, my parents would be devastated, and Wade, as much as I hadn't yet forgiven him for insulting my vintage obsession, would probably harbor guilt for the rest of his life.

Not to mention that I wouldn't get to finish my degree in forensic science or have a date with Grant Tilney. No one would be around to help my little sister Anna get through high school. All my life plans would come to naught—the house I wanted to build, the children I wanted to raise, the vacations I'd imagined. It all seemed like a nightmare, and, though my palms grew sweaty and my heart pounded, I almost couldn't believe that it was real. But it was real, and I needed to do something about it.

I tried to reason with Ingrid once again. "I swear I'm not Leslie Kaplan. I just saw the name written down on a notepad. I have no idea who she is or what she does. I don't know her at all. I promise. You can search the internet. My name's Eva Morland. You can ask Grant."

Ingrid turned to look out the window as if she hadn't heard anything I said. This was just her job, and she clearly wasn't a people person.

"Do you even know Grant Tilney?"

Again, she didn't answer.

How had I stumbled into this mess? "I mean it," I yelled. "There's gonna be hell to pay if you don't let me go. I'm not someone you can mess with."

Nothing but silence came from the front seat.

Fine. I could make my plan without them. The next time Ronald stopped the car, which he'd have to do at some point, I'd dive over the front seat, knock out Ingrid, and escape through her door.

The problem was that the drive went on for two more hours, so instead of escaping, I thought of all the things I was going to do after I escaped. I was speculating that it might be possible to have my own fashion line within a year when Ronald turned the car onto a dirt road that led through dry grasslands.

I was expecting a large metal placard announcing the name of the ranch. Instead, this was just a gap in a barbed wire fence and a dirt road that went on for miles. Fields of dry grass stretched on either side of us as we jostled over bumps and dips in the road.

After two or three miles of driving, I decided escape might not be possible—at least not on foot the way I'd imagined.

I'd need a vehicle.

After another mile or two, we pulled up to a dumpy white trailer with a rickety porch built from two-by-fours. It was a horror movie waiting to happen, and every logical thought disappeared from my brain.

This was where they planned to kill me. Not that I would let them.

Once Ronald pulled the car around to the side of the trailer, I saw a single black Jeep parked behind it. That meant there would be someone else I'd have to fight off inside the trailer. I had to act now.

When Ronald opened my door, I kneed him right between the legs. He doubled over, and I ran back to the dirt road, but Ingrid was already coming after me. She grabbed onto my hair and pulled.

"No fair," I yelled, a reaction from my childhood when my parents had strict rules about hair pulling. I grasped her hands and pulled in the opposite direction, but Ronald grabbed onto my arms, and they both dragged me to the trailer as I fell to the ground, screaming and kicking and digging my nails into Ronald's wrists as panic overrode all my logical thoughts.

They dragged me up the steps—Ingrid pulling me by the hair and Ronald pulling my arms.

I squirmed and kicked as they dragged me over the threshold and onto the dirty orange linoleum. I hadn't been inside many trailer homes, just the double-wide my grandmother lived in. This one seemed much smaller, and it reeked of cigarette smoke. Ronald pulled me past a refrigerator and stove. Then he tried to lift me onto a folding chair, but I grabbed onto his legs, immobilizing him as best I could.

"Mrs. Garland," Ingrid called in her harsh foreign accent. She was breathless from the fight, but she still had a hold on my hair. "We've arrived."

A door opened on the other side of the room, and a tall woman with long black hair emerged. She was dressed like an old-time rodeo queen in a flared denim skirt and peasant blouse along with red cowboy boots. If she hadn't been one of my kidnappers, I would have complimented her style. "Y'all made good time," she said in a slow, Southern drawl. "I barely got here myself." I could tell her hair was dyed just by the wrinkles around her eyes and mouth. No woman that age could possibly have hair that dark.

"I'm happy we didn't waste any more of your time than necessary, Mrs. Garland," Ronald cooed, bowing his head.

How did she have such power over him that he was willing to kidnap me? And why did she want to kidnap me—or Leslie—in the first place?

Mrs. Garland looked me up and down. "I didn't expect Ms. Kaplan to be so young."

Again with the Leslie Kaplan thing. I should have never made that mistake. "I keep telling them," I yelled, trying to pull my hair from Ingrid's grip. "I'm not Leslie Kaplan. I only said I was so I could see Grant."

"She's tricky," Ingrid said, yanking my hair even harder. "As soon as she fell into our trap, it was all naiveté. Part of her disguise, I suppose. You cannot trust anything she says, and she wears gloves so she doesn't leave fingerprints."

"Well, we'll just have to pull out all the stops," Mrs. Garland said, pointing to the folding chair. "Tie her up, Ronald."

I tried to explain how I'd come looking for Grant Tilney and had seen the note on the desk, but Ronald was already shoving me into the chair. The good part about that was that Ingrid finally had to let go of my hair. There was no way I was going to let them tie me down, though. I fought back with everything I had, kicking and squirming until Mrs. Garland yelled, "If you don't settle down, I'm going to have to bite you." Then she sat on my lap, her bony butt digging into my thighs while Ingrid fastened my wrists and ankles to the chair with zip ties.

They'd used the thin kind of zip ties, which was pretty unprofessional in my opinion. My siblings and I had once tied each other up with the thickest zip ties we could find. (Growing up in the country, we'd tried just about everything we could think of for entertainment.) I knew exactly how to escape—if I could just get my teeth on the things.

Once they had me properly confined, Mrs. Garland opened the cabinet and pulled out one of those fumigators you get at the store—my mom always called them bug bombs. It's that can of spray that you set off to kill all the bugs in your house at once. Since my parents weren't fans of pesticides—we raised our own organic produce—I didn't have any experience with fumigators. I only knew that I couldn't stand to walk down the pesticide aisle at the hardware store—the heavy scent always nauseated me, and I could imagine the acrid scent of the poison inside the can as she waved it in front of my face.

She fingered the release button on top of the can. "I have a few questions to ask you before I set this off. Whether or not you get to leave depends on how well you answer. Think of this as a test with consequences. You give me the answers I want. I let you out of here before the bomb goes off."

"Seriously? You're threatening me with a bug bomb?" I tried to sound tough but I was scared spit-less.

Mrs. Garland strode over to the cabinet and threw it open, revealing a shelf full of bug bombs. "Not one. Ten. If you happen to survive, you'll still be too sick to make it back to the highway. The only way you're getting back to your normal, charmed life is by answering my questions. First, I'll need the name of your informant."

I was all for answering the questions and getting back to my charmed life. The problem was that I didn't know any names, and I didn't want to get anyone in trouble.

I said the first made-up name that came to mind. "My informant? I know him as Leland Stottlemeyer, but that might have been a code name. I'm not sure."

Mrs. Garland narrowed her eyes and waved the can in front of my face. "You think I don't watch TV? That's the captain on *Monk*. You're going to have to do better than that."

"I told you it was a code name. I don't know his real name."

"I'm not buying it." She set the bug bomb on the table in front of me. Then she went to the cabinet and got another and another until all ten of them sat in front of me. "I want real names."

I bit my lip. "How do I know you're not going to kill me anyway?"

"You'll just have to trust me. You give me a real name, not a code name; I make sure you get back to Houston alive."

That was exactly what I wanted—to get back to Houston alive. I'd already caused my parents enough grief by flunking out of gym and deciding to major in forensic science.

I had to think of a name. If Leland Stottlemeyer didn't work, Norman Bates and Caroline Bingley likely wouldn't either. I had to give her a real name. I had to buy some time. "Can I tell you without those other two here?"

She shook her head. "What's good enough for my ears is good enough for theirs."

I lifted my chin, motioning as best as I could for her to come closer. "Ingrid," I whispered. "She's the one who's been telling me all about the inner workings of your organization. She's given us names, numbers …"

Ronald glared at Ingrid. "That would explain a lot."

Ingrid trembled, folding her arms as she looked from Ronald to Mrs. Garland. "She's bluffing. You know I'm completely loyal."

I thought of all the boxes I'd seen at the warehouse. "She told us about the next delivery."

Ronald brought a hand to his forehead, raking his fingers through his hair. "The next delivery?" He walked to the door, pulling out his phone. "I'll have to call the driver."

"They plan to intercept it before it gets to the border," I said.

Mrs. Garland eyed me as she worked her jaw from side to side. "Which border?"

I couldn't risk hesitation. I had to keep talking as quick as the thoughts came. "The Texas border. I gave them the schedule."

Mrs. Garland folded her arms. "You're being too vague. I don't believe you." With that, she pulled off the safety seal on the bug bomb and pressed the button. A hazy white fog emerged. "Give me specifics."

I held my breath as the acrid gas filled the trailer. Ingrid and Ronald rushed toward the cabinet and pulled out a package of face masks. They looked a lot like the kind my family used for painting and sanding.

"You give me details, or I'll set off the other nine." Mrs. Garland said as she put on her mask.

"No." I pushed as hard as I could with my legs and managed to scoot my chair back a few inches.

She picked up another bug bomb and choked. "You bought the wrong kind of mask," she shouted to Ingrid and Ronald. "These aren't working." Ingrid and Ronald rushed forward, both covering their mouths. "Set off the bombs fast, so we can get out of here." I scooted my chair back another few inches as they set off three more cans at once, enveloping themselves in a fog.

I could see how clever this plan was. The coroner would probably rule my death as an accidental poisoning, thinking I was simply trying to rid this place of cockroaches. I could feel myself succumbing to the fumes. My thoughts grew hazy as I struggled to breathe. At least, it would be quick. I wouldn't have to suffer long.

CHAPTER 3

I couldn't let myself die. I was too stubborn for that. Little by little, and hidden in the smog of the bug bomb, I continued scooting my chair toward the open door, praying that somehow Ingrid and Ronald wouldn't notice. They were still setting off bombs as fast as they could, each one erupting with a *ffffttt* while Mrs. Garland was choking in the doorway. The more I wriggled in my chair, the more I could move my arms through the zip ties. I'd surely be able to get my teeth on one of the ties soon.

Ingrid spoke through the haze. "I'm starting to feel—" Her words broke off, and I heard a thud.

Straining to peer through the cloud of pesticide, I saw her lying on the floor beside the table. Ronald lay beside her, unconscious on the floor.

Having been farther away from the bombs and sitting closer to the floor, I must have been shielded from their effects. Here I'd been thinking these people were evil geniuses to kill me this way, but I'd been wrong. They were incompetent criminals. All I had to do now was get to the door and bite off my zip ties— in whatever order worked best.

If only Mrs. Garland wasn't standing in the doorway. "Oh no you don't," she yelled, but she ended up choking. "You stay," she said, gasping for breath, "where you are"

Fine. I'd stay where I was. But while she walked out on the porch, coughing, I bit the end of each zip tie to loosen it and slid my hands free. Mrs. Garland wouldn't be able to see me well through the fog, not that she was trying.

All I had to do now was get the zip ties off my ankles before she noticed my arms were free. My eyes were watering so much, I could barely see, but I bent down to feel the chair legs. That's when I realized that Ingrid had attached the zip ties below the horizontal bar that connected the chair legs. All I had to do to free myself was to rock backward in my folding chair and slip the zip ties off of the chair's feet. I wouldn't be free of the zip ties, but I would be free of the chair.

Now, all I had to do was get past the porch, where Mrs. Garland stood.

I glanced around for some type of weapon—a heavy vase or a wrench perhaps. There was nothing. The countertops were bare.

Then I realized I already had a weapon, my chair. While Mrs. Garland coughed on the porch, I stood, folding the chair up flat. Turning it upside-down and holding onto the legs, I swung it above me. Then I walked out the door, hitting Mrs. Garland so hard on top of the head that she fell forward onto her hands and knees on the porch.

I stepped over her, and as I did, I noticed that she was holding onto a big, black purse.

I grabbed it, thinking it might contain keys to the Jeep that was parked out front. Right then, I needed keys as much as I needed fresh air. I was in the middle of nowhere, after all. If I hoped to live through this, I'd need a way to escape. My life depended on getting that purse.

It was at least as big as my college backpack but much heavier, and she kept hold of it, so that the harder I pulled, the more I pulled her up from where she'd fallen.

We had a tug of war, both of us pulling back and forth on the purse. Wrinkle creams, earrings, lipsticks, and nail polish flew every which way, but no keys. That's when it struck me that this was probably a newer car. If the keys were inside the purse, the door might open without me pressing down on the fob.

All I needed to do was get the purse away from her. Since the tug of war was a draw, I tried shaking the purse from side to side. As I did, I advanced my grip, grabbing onto the body of the purse instead of just the handle.

Out flew her phone, then a tin of breath mints, one of those big planner books, and something that looked like a sleeve of Thin Mints. I saw her eyes dart to the side—following the cookies, and I took the opportunity to yank as hard as I could, finally pulling the purse free.

Taking my chances that the key was inside the purse, I ran as fast as I could for the Jeep. I could hear Mrs. Garland's footsteps behind me as I yanked on the driver's side door handle. It opened. Swinging the door open only as far as I needed, I slipped into the driver's seat as she grabbed onto the skirt of my dress. As soon as I got my feet inside, I slammed the door shut on my dress. Mrs. Garland was right there, holding onto the other side of the handle so it wouldn't shut.

With one hand, I pushed down on the lock button, trying to get the door to lock. It wouldn't. Then I pressed the start button on the Jeep. Nothing.

I couldn't give up. I was so close to getting away. But I couldn't hold onto the door with just one hand much longer. She was pulling too hard. I had to hold on with both hands.

This was getting me nowhere. I just wanted to be done with her, and yet I couldn't move or get away, so I did what came naturally when someone was being rude. Dropping my head into the center of the steering wheel, I honked the horn.

For a second, Mrs. Garland startled, and as soon as I felt her hold on the door weaken, I pressed the lock button again. This time it worked. I was safe.

I pressed the start button again, remembering to put my foot on the brake as I pressed it. The car roared to life, and country music blared from the radio. I'd always wanted to drive a Jeep, and this one seemed to have just the engine I needed today. I slid the gear shift to reverse and backed away from the trailer. Mrs. Garland was still hanging onto the side of the Jeep, shouting for me to stop.

"I hope you're not planning to abandon your friends in the trailer," I shouted back. Anger had replaced my fear of this woman. She didn't care about anyone other than herself, and if she kept hanging onto the side of this Jeep, I was going to take her for the ride she deserved.

I floored the gas and peeled backward. That took care of Mrs. Garland. As I turned the Jeep forward, I saw she was heading back for the trailer.

Maybe that meant she wasn't as wicked as I'd thought. She was going to save her friends. Still, I was anxious to put some distance between us. I pushed down on the gas pedal and raced back to the dirt road. But before I'd gotten even a hundred yards down the road, I glanced up at the rearview mirror and saw that Mrs. Garland was coming out of the trailer, heading for the sedan. Likely, the only reason she'd gone inside was to get the keys from Ronald.

I pushed down on the gas even harder, liking the feel of bumping over the dirt ruts as the speedometer rose to thirty, forty, and then fifty. Surely, this Jeep could outrace a sedan. I glanced down at the controls and finally let myself lean against the back of the seat. I had three-quarters of a tank of gas! I was home free.

I had done it—I'd freed myself from zip-ties, escaped fumigation, and fought off an attacker. Wade was never going to believe it—Poor Wade! He was probably worried about me.

I hoped he hadn't told Mom and Dad I'd disappeared.

Not that there was anything I could do about it now. I was in the middle of nowhere. On either side of the dirt road, fields of dry grass stretched for miles. I'd have to wait to call them until I had access to a phone.

What would my family think when they found out what had happened?

Those people had tried to kill me. They didn't even know me … and they wanted me dead.

Tears blurred my vision, so I blinked them back as I drove over the rutted road, leaving a cloud of dust behind the Jeep. I couldn't let my guard down now. For all I knew, Mrs. Garland was right behind me in the sedan.

I held my jaw tight, trying to keep my teeth from clicking together as I drove over the bumps. Instinctively, I reached for the stereo, which was tuned to the news. I needed music, and luckily, the Jeep had satellite radio with tons of song choices, even out here in the Podunks. I settled on "I Will Survive" by Gloria Gaynor and started to sing along. How serendipitous that it came on just now. I had survived a kidnapping.

I sang that song and then three more. I'd been going forty-five miles per hour for at least ten minutes now. There was no way Mrs. Garland could go that fast in a sedan on a dirt road.

In my frazzled state, I threw together a plan. I would drive as fast as I could until I either got pulled over, or I reached a public place. My first priority was to call an ambulance for Ingrid and Ronald. Yes, they'd kidnapped me, but I couldn't let them die or, worse, escape. I'd make sure the police knew about all three of them—Ronald, Ingrid, and Mrs. Garland. They were all three murderers and kidnappers, who needed to be brought to justice.

After that, I'd call my family. And, after that, I'd use the bathroom. It had been hours since I'd had that large cream soda. On second thought, maybe I'd use the bathroom first.

It was hard to believe this was all happening. In the space of one afternoon, I'd met the man of my dreams. Then I'd been kidnapped, someone had tried to kill me, and I'd stolen a Jeep. I played the story over in my mind as I drove, wondering how my friends would react when they saw me on the news.

Finally, I turned onto the freeway, where I took note of the mile post—346—before speeding up even faster. This was an emergency, after all.

I passed a few cars and trucks. Buildings were harder to find. I drove for what seemed like hours before I found a place to stop—although looking at the clock, it had only been about twenty minutes.

It was a little gas station called The Hole in the Wall. The first thing I did after parking and walking inside was ask to use the phone. The woman behind the counter, who looked about my mom's age but had dyed her hair bright green, handed me the receiver. "There's a five-minute limit." She had on a bright pink tank top that revealed her ample curves.

"Okay." All I wanted was to get this over with, so I could relieve my bladder.

I heaved Mrs. Garland's big black purse onto the counter and punched 911 into the phone. The dispatcher answered. "911. What is your emergency?" It was a male voice.

"Hi, um. This is Eva Morland. Someone may have reported my kidnapping." I crossed my legs. Maybe I should have gone to the bathroom first. The green-haired lady leaned forward across the counter, her eyes wide. "I've escaped in my kidnappers' car.

But I'm kind of worried about two of them. They've been poisoned by bug bombs."

"I'm sorry?" the dispatcher said. "Did you say bug bombs?"

"That's right," I said, catching sight of the restroom sign at the back of the store. "Bug bombs … or fumigators. I think that's the official name for them."

"May I remind you that it's a crime to prank call 911?" The dispatcher's voice had developed a hard edge. "If you're about to deliver a line about cockroaches, you might as well hang up right now."

I really needed to go to the bathroom. "I promise this isn't about bugs. A man and woman—Ingrid and Ronald—took me to a trailer out in the middle of nowhere. There was another woman there, named Mrs. Garland, and she had them set off ten bug bombs to try and poison me, but Ingrid and Ronald didn't get out of the trailer fast enough. I think they need medical attention."

A long pause followed before the dispatcher asked, "What is your location?"

"Excuse me a moment. I've got to ask the sales clerk." I covered the receiver and asked the green-haired lady for the location.

"Hole in the Wall gas station," she said, "mile post 365 on Route 485."

I repeated the location to the dispatcher and then added, "But the people who need immediate help for the poisoning are in a different location. I had to come here to use the phone."

"Where is the location of the poison victims?"

"They're in a trailer that's on a dirt road near mile post 346 on Route 485. They need an ambulance."

I had to go to the bathroom so bad, I was dancing back and forth while they asked my name and home address. I also gave them Mrs. Garland's license plate number and her description. Then I went through the whole story of my kidnapping, giving descriptions of Ingrid and Ronald.

"Listen," I finally said, "I really have to go to the bathroom. Can we continue this conversation after I get back?"

"All right, ma'am. Let me talk to the store clerk while you're off the phone."

I handed the phone to the green-haired lady and made a dash for the restroom. As I got to the back of the store, I could hear the green-haired lady speaking into the phone. "She doesn't look crazy, but you never know. She is dressed a little strange."

"You should talk," I muttered as I flung open the restroom door. I could have defended myself, but I had more pressing matters to attend to. Once the police got there, they would see how it was. All they had to do was follow that dirt road to the trailer and find those two lying comatose on the linoleum. Then they'd believe me. Not only that, my story would be all over the news ... which meant I might get some publicity for my vlogs without having to die.

When I emerged from the restroom, the green-haired lady was still talking on the phone. "I'll keep her here for you." She glanced my way and flashed me a smile. "Here she is again." She handed me back the phone.

"I'm sending an officer," the dispatcher said. "It might be a while. You're pretty far from the station, but just sit tight. He'll get there as soon as he can."

"Thank you," I said. Then I hung up.

The green-haired lady dispensed a Blue Raspberry Icee into an extra-large paper cup, stuck a red straw into it, and pushed it across the counter to me. "Here, you look like you could use this."

It was true. I smiled and thanked her, noticing for the first time that her nametag read Loretta.

I leaned on the counter and slurped up the slush. Not only was that pesticide probably going to give me cancer, it made me crave carbs like nothing else. I had made it to the bottom of the drink and my straw was about to make that rude noise that always upset Mom when I remembered—my brother. He probably thought I was still being kidnapped. I turned to Loretta "I know I've already used my five minutes on the phone, but I forgot to tell my brother that I'm okay, and I'm betting it's long distance to call him from here."

"It's no problem, honey," she said, extracting her personal cell phone from her back pocket. "I'll let you use my cell … for as long as you want."

"Thank you!"

Wade answered on the first ring. "Hi."

"Hey, it's Eva. I'm sorry if you've been worried. A couple of crazy people tried to kidnap me, but I'm totally safe now. I just need to talk to the police. Then I'll be heading back to Houston … I might need a ride though."

"You know Clayton spent thirty dollars on your ticket to the escape room." His words grated with anger. "You could have at least let us know you weren't going to come." He was in full-on lecture mode, speaking fast and furious.

"Have you heard anything I just said? I got kidnapped, Wade. Somebody tried to kill me. I just barely escaped."

I could hear him exhale. "If you didn't want to go on a date with my roommate, you should have just said so instead of inventing a ridiculous story."

I placed a hand on my hip and raised my voice. "It's not a ridiculous story. It's a true story. I met a guy in the café while I was waiting for you. When he left, he took my phone instead of his, so I went looking for him. But instead of finding the guy, I met two people who threw me in a car and took me out to the middle of nowhere. Then they tried to poison me with bug bombs." I paused, waiting for his apology.

The green-haired lady was pretending to read a Family Circle magazine, but I could tell she wasn't reading a thing.

"That seems like a lot of trouble just to get out of a blind date," Wade said. Mom had once called him her most intelligent child. Boy, had he ever pulled the wool over her eyes.

"I didn't plan to get kidnapped, Wade. It just happened."

"You've been watching too many detective shows." He laughed. "You could have done a better job of leaving clues. I had no idea what was going on. Who did you bring along to help you drop the truck off at that warehouse? But honestly, it was a really low blow to stand Clayton up. He was looking forward to meeting you."

"This isn't a joke, Wade. I've spent the last couple hours thinking I might die, and you know what? I felt really bad because I thought you'd feel guilty that I went missing when I was supposed to be meeting you. But obviously, I shouldn't have felt bad for you at all. You don't seem to have any feelings, at least not for me." I really wanted to hang up on him at that point, but I just had to make one more point. "You know what? I'm going to have the police officer talk to you once he gets here. Then you're going to feel terrible that you're giving me such a hard time." With that, I hung up the phone. He'd be sorry when I ended up on the evening news tonight. This was going to be huge. These people were probably in some big drug trafficking ring, and I was going to help the police break the case.

While I still had Loretta's cell phone, I tried calling my phone to see if Grant would answer it. It rang a few times, but no one answered.

Loretta snapped her gum and shook her head. "You're in quite the pickle. It reminds me of my second marriage."

For the next half hour, I got to hear about Loretta's second marriage. While she went on to explain about her third, I dug through the black purse. I didn't find any identification, but I did find a gold necklace with the name Donna on it. That had to be her name—Donna Garland.

Loretta was telling me about her fourth marriage when a police car finally pulled to a stop in front of the place.

Instead of coming right in, the officer walked over to look at the Jeep that I'd driven from the trailer. He looked to be around thirty years old, had dark hair, and was as skinny as a rodeo rider. I went outside to meet him. "Hi," I said. "I'm Eva Morland. The dispatcher sent you here to talk to me."

"Yes," he said, fingering his mustache, "but I couldn't help noticing this car here. It was reported stolen."

"Well, that's probably because I used it to escape from my kidnappers this afternoon."

He shook his head and narrowed his eyes at me. "Nope. It was reported stolen last week from Houston."

I had the feeling he didn't believe me, which made me want to rub my neck or crack my knuckles, but I didn't want to look nervous. He'd never believe me if I looked nervous. "Ronald and Ingrid must have stolen it. They're the ones that were poisoned in that trailer near mile post 346."

His eyes bore right through me. "There weren't any poison victims in the trailer by milepost 346."

"The trailer wasn't right there on the highway. You have to follow a dirt road up a few miles to find it."

"Believe me, ma'am, I followed the dirt road before the ambulance got there. I found the trailer, but no one was there. We busted down the door because we'd received the emergency call, but we didn't find anyone inside. It did smell a little funny, but I didn't find any bug bombs." His voice was rough and deep.

I bit the side of my lip. "I promise I'm telling the truth, sir." Then I remembered the big black purse and held it out to him. "This was my kidnapper's purse. I took it from her."

Shaking his head, he took the purse and then blew out his breath, letting his lips flap. "Maybe you'd better drive out there to the trailer with me, just to make sure I got the right place. I didn't smell any kind of fumigation."

After he put the black purse in his trunk, he opened the passenger side door for me, and I slid inside, taking a good look at his laptop and radio equipment. As we pulled onto the freeway, he turned on his flashing lights. "Because hopefully this really is an emergency," he told me.

"You'll see," I told him. "It sounds crazy, but I'm telling the truth." While we drove, I told him the whole story, starting at the café where Grant and I accidentally exchanged phones. Then I told him about trying to find Grant at the warehouse, where I read the name Leslie Kaplan and Ingrid forced me into the car.

"Do you think you could figure out the address of that warehouse?" the officer asked.

"I could if I had my phone."

He took a phone from his front pocket and handed it to me. "Could you find it on my phone?"

That's when I knew he was finally on my side. "Yes," I said.

The officer's internet service was super slow, which was to be expected so far out in the country, but after a few minutes, I figured out the address of the warehouse. "It's 288 B Bootleg Rd. in Houston."

"Good," he said. He called it into the dispatcher on his police radio. "I've got a 60 at the Hole in the Wall. On route to a possible 27. And I'm gonna need a 70 on 288 B Bootleg Rd for a possible number 4. Ms. Morland here says her purse is still there. It sounds like the place may have something to do with our 60."

Now that the officer was on my side, I was sure we were going to get Mrs. Garland and the others to pay for their crimes. The police would go to the warehouse, find my purse, and check out whatever was in those boxes.

By the time we made it to the dirt road, the sun was beginning to set in the sky. I could still see the tracks from the sedan and the Jeep, right there in the dirt, along with a few more tracks that must have come from the officer's car and the ambulance. They seemed to have come down the right road.

We drove and drove. "I think it's coming up soon," I told the officer. "This is definitely the right road."

It was dusk by the time we arrived at the trailer. This time, though, there was an old brown truck beside it. "This is it," I said. "But the truck wasn't here before."

"Stay in the car," the officer said as he got out, his hand over his gun.

As he approached the little porch, the storm door opened, and an old man with a long, gray beard hobbled out. He wasn't anyone I'd seen before and I scrunched down in my seat, wondering if he might be in league with Mrs. Garland.

The old man shook his head over and over as the officer spoke with him, and after a while, he pointed at me and began yelling something about how I'd been heckling him, but it was all in Spanish, so I only caught about half of what I supposedly had said. Then he went back inside his trailer, trying to slam his broken door, which just bounced back open.

34

The officer walked back to the car and spent a few minutes filling out a form on his laptop. While he was doing that, I got out of the car and walked to the side of the house, where there was a metal trash can. Lifting the lid, I peeked inside. There were the bug bombs—all ten of them.

I motioned for the officer to come join me and then pointed to the canisters. "Did the man say anything about the bug bombs."

The officer raised his brows and shook his head. "No, and he doesn't know anyone named Mrs. Garland or Ingrid or Ronald." He took a photo with his phone. "I'll put this in the report when we get back to the station."

It took us another half hour to arrive back at the tiny police station. It was around nine P.M. by the time we got there. My officer was going off duty, so I had to wait on a hard chair for the next officer to come talk to me. All I wanted was to crawl back into my bed back home on the farm—three hours away.

The officer who came to file my report was a young, blond man, who looked like he could have been in eighth grade—except for the mustache. After he took down my whole story, he said, "The guys in Houston checked out your warehouse. Apparently, there was no one there all day except the manager. All the employees were at a Home Remodeling Expo in Austin. The manager didn't find your purse, and when the Houston officers asked him about Ronald and Ingrid, he said he didn't know anyone by those names."

I groaned inside, knowing this guy probably thought I'd fabricated the whole story. I'd heard of people who did things like that to get attention on social media. "Is there some way you can track Grant Tilney's phone?" I asked. "It's probably still in that warehouse. Or you could search the hospitals to see if there were any cases of bug bomb poisoning."

The blond officer cleared his throat as he looked down at his notepad. "I'll make a note of Mr. Tilney in the report before I finish filing it." In other words, he wanted to get rid of me. I heard that police officers often had to deal with people who lied to get attention. Why wouldn't they think I was a liar too?

"Can you test my skin for pesticide residue?" I asked.

"And what would it prove if we found pesticide residue?" he asked. "You can find pesticide at any drug or grocery store you walk into."

He was right, but there had to be some way I could prove that I'd actually been kidnapped. I flopped over, letting my head rest on my knees. It was then I noticed that I still had the zip ties around my ankles. "Look! They tied me up with these!"

He stared down at my ankle as his lips twisted. "I'll collect those for evidence."

It almost seemed that he thought I was the criminal, instead of the one who'd been kidnapped.

CHAPTER 4

I woke up the next morning to the sound of a guy singing in my brother's kitchen. I'd ended up calling Wade to pick me up from the police station, and I'd been so tired by the time he picked me up that I decided to crash on his couch instead of driving home. "Clayton's making you eggs and bacon," Wade whispered, leaning over me as I lay on the couch. I was still wearing my blue taffeta dress. "Pretty forgiving of him, considering that you stood him up yesterday just to play your little mystery novel prank."

I heaved a sigh. We'd already had this discussion the night before. Obviously, a good night's sleep had done nothing to improve his thinking skills. "It wasn't a prank," I said, preparing myself to renew my argument, but Wade was already leaving the room. I raised my voice. "My phone is gone. My dress is filthy. And I smell like pesticides—even though I showered. Do you really think I would fake all this?"

Then it hit me—maybe Wade was the one who was faking. I'd suspected he might be involved the day before. After all, the whole situation was ridiculous. Maybe he had engineered all of it—sending Grant to the diner with a phone identical to mine, telling the server to send me around the corner to a warehouse, getting Ingrid to kidnap me, and arranging for some fake bug bombs in an old trailer.

I supposed he could have pulled all of that off. But what about the police officers and the stolen car? He couldn't have faked that. It had to be real.

I followed Wade into the kitchen, where someone had set the table with an assortment of mismatched plastic plates and cups. My anger melted away as I saw a guy standing at the stove, a spatula in his hand. He wasn't bad looking—a little on the skinny side but still tall, dark, and handsome. So this was Clayton. "I'm sorry I didn't make it for our date yesterday," I said. "I really was looking forward to it." It wasn't exactly a lie. I had been looking forward to the escape room and to seeing how Wade reacted to my

Grace Kelly get-up. "It would have been much more fun than being kidnapped."

He smiled. "Sorry you had such a rough day." The glimmer in his eye suggested he was playing along with a game rather than expressing sympathy. "Maybe I could help you solve your kidnapping mystery after we eat breakfast."

"I'd like that." At least he was willing to listen to my story, even if his tone of voice annoyed me.

Over our eggs and bacon, I told him how I'd met Grant in the diner and how I'd gone looking for him after he accidentally took my phone. I gasped. His phone! "I just realized, Grant's phone is still at that warehouse. I need to get in touch with him and apologize."

"I think it's more important that you prove your story about this whole kidnapping thing. Those people sound terrible." Clayton spoke in a dramatic tone, as if he were speaking to a child. "We should go back to that warehouse and see if we can find your purse."

"No way am I going back in there. They can keep my purse. I've already called to cancel my cards." The truck was probably still parked there, but I'd let Wade take care of that later.

"But you're missing out on a great opportunity as a vlogger. I could help you record a video about your experience, and I'd be there to protect you in case something else happens."

He had a point about the vlogging opportunity. "Shouldn't I try to contact Grant first? He has to be wondering how he can get his phone back."

Clayton shook his head. "Nah. You don't even know his last name."

"But I do. It's Tilney."

Clayton grew quiet and took out his phone. I thought he was going to look for Grant's number, but all he did was check the weather. "We should go to the warehouse while the lighting is good. Morning light is the best for filming, and it's already past nine."

I was beginning to wonder if he might be a little bit jealous of Grant Tilney to keep changing the subject away from him. I hadn't said anything about how handsome Grant was or how we'd shared a natural rapport, but it must have been obvious in my expression. I never was good at hiding my emotions. "I guess we could do that," I said, "but I can't vlog without my phone."

"We can use my phone," Clayton said. "It makes great videos."

He was right. This story could be the break I needed for my vlog. There was just one problem. I held out the skirt on my dress. "I'm going to need a new outfit." I wished I'd brought a change of clothes with me. "I could pick something up at a thrift store, but I don't have any money."

"Oh," Wade called out as if he'd been listening from the other room. "I can loan you some money."

Clayton didn't think there were any thrift stores nearby, but Wade let us know about one right down the street. He handed me a twenty-dollar bill, and then Clayton walked me to his sleek black convertible. I would have enjoyed my ride immensely if Clayton hadn't taken the opportunity to fill me in on all the details about his stereo system, engine, and tires. After my experience the day before, I wasn't too anxious to drive around with the top down either. I wanted the doors locked and all the windows up.

We went to the thrift store first, where I had to decide between a garnet evening gown and a flowered chintz dress. After seeing the look of approval Clayton gave me when I tried on the gown, I decided on the flowered chintz dress, along with a killer pair of red sunglasses, and a pair of long gloves. After all, Clayton wasn't my date for the prom. Our time together was all about business.

"Do you have to wear the gloves?" Clayton asked. "They're kind of weird."

I smiled as I slipped them on. "They're my signature style."

After I bought my outfit, we drove to the diner. The staff was all different, so we couldn't interview my server from the day before, but Clayton interviewed me as I sat at a booth in the corner. Then we drove to the warehouse parking lot and took some footage of Dad's old truck, which was still there. I wished I could just hop right in and head home right then, but Clayton was so enthusiastic about our vlogging project, and I had to admit, it would be nice to have some video evidence of what I'd experienced.

Next, while I stayed in the car taking video with Clayton's phone, Clayton pounded on the warehouse door that Ronald had opened the day before. After just a few minutes, a woman answered, but she wasn't Ingrid. She was younger and blond. I clicked the door locks on Clayton's car and held my breath while Clayton spoke to her. Their conversation went on for a few minutes, and she seemed to be shrugging a lot, but she did write something down on a notecard for him.

After she closed the door, he waved the notecard in the air as he walked back to the car. I unlocked the door right before he pulled it open. "You really do look nervous," he said, laughing. "If I didn't know better—"

"If you didn't know better, what?" I growled.

"Never mind." He smiled and glanced over at his phone, which I still held. "Did you get some good footage?"

"Let me check," I said, figuring I could maybe sneak a call in to my old phone. "What did she write on that notecard?"

"An address," he said, handing me the card as he pulled out of the parking lot. "She said it's the person who owns the warehouse. Funny she didn't give me a phone number, don't you think?"

"Yeah," I said, looking at the neat handwriting. "Do you care if I look it up on your phone?"

"Go ahead." He turned right, heading toward route 389. "Are you ready to head out to that trailer now?"

I typed the address into Clayton's phone and waited until the directions came up. "The owner of the warehouse only lives eight minutes away."

Clayton pulled the car to the side of the road and took his phone from me, looking at the directions. "We should go there," he said, flashing me a grin.

"I don't know," I said, figuring there was a good chance that at least one of my kidnappers lived there. "I'd rather give the address to the police."

But he was already turning the car around. "You can stay in the car. Tell me what their boss looked like again."

I described Mrs. Garland in detail—the dark dyed hair, the wrinkles around her eyes, the pasty white skin, the heavy Southern accent, and the rodeo-style clothing. Clayton asked me some more questions about the bug bombs, and, because he was a pre-med major, he launched into what he would have done to save Ingrid and Ronald. I suppressed a yawn. "I can tell you're going to be a great doctor."

The house was only about twenty minutes away in a community with enormous homes, the kind that had little waterfall ponds in the front and swimming pools in the back. Instead of having a waterfall pond in the front, though, this one had a statue of a jaguar that sent an icy chill down my spine.

"Can we please go now? I've seen enough." My kidnappers wanted me dead, after all, and it wasn't like Clayton would protect me if they caught sight of me again. He just saw this whole thing as a game.

Clayton frowned, turning to me as he parked the car along the street. "You were the one who put the address into my phone."

"That didn't mean I wanted to knock on the door."

He shrugged. "I'll go myself then." He got out of his car and pulled out his phone to take a video as he walked up to ring the doorbell.

That's when a bloodcurdling scream pierced the air. It was so loud, I could hear it with the car windows rolled up.

I expected Clayton to go searching for whoever was screaming, but the front door of the house opened, and he started talking to a silver-haired woman I'd never seen before.

I rolled down the window. "I think someone needs help," I yelled to Clayton.

She screamed again.

"Did you hear that?" I called.

Clayton turned from the woman at the front door. "She says it's just a peacock," he yelled.

41

A peacock? It could be … but it could also be a woman in danger. I wasn't about to let someone else suffer the way I had. If only I had Clayton's phone with me, I could call for help.

Another scream broke through my thoughts. It seemed to be coming from the back of the house.

Clayton still stood at the door, talking to the woman. He wasn't going to help. I would have to do this on my own.

Taking a deep breath, I burst out of the car and ran down a flagstone path that led to the backyard.

"Do you need help?" I called out as I came to a tall cedar fence.

"Stay away from me!" a woman shouted from behind the fence.

She couldn't have meant me. I'd just gotten there. She was being attacked by someone else. I needed a weapon. Glancing around, I saw a terracotta frog and picked it up. Though it was large, it was much lighter than it looked, but it was all I had.

Holding the frog above my head with one hand, I pushed open the gate with the other. Out of the corner of my eye, I saw a man racing across the grass on the other side of the pool. It was the same man who'd been in the trailer when the policeman took me back there—the old man. Only now that he was running, he didn't seem so old.

"Clayton," I yelled. "Help!"

And there, right in front of me stood Ingrid. She had to be the one who'd screamed, but she wasn't in trouble at all. In fact, she was laughing. This was a trap. They'd given us the address, so we'd come here, and now they were trying to kidnap me again.

I brought the frog statue down on her head as hard as I could. She brought her hands up in defense, but it was too late. She crumpled to the ground, unconscious. I hadn't expected that, given that the statue was so light.

Had I really hurt her? She was so still.

I studied her, making sure it wasn't just my imagination that her chest seemed to be rising and falling.

Then I saw the red leather. She had a purse in her hand— my purse, the one I'd left in the warehouse.

As I snatched the purse away, a man burst out the backdoor. "What's going on?" he cried.

I gasped. "I don't know," I said, "I just got here."

But the man had already pulled out a gun, and it was pointed right at me.

CHAPTER 5

I held up my hands, still gripping my purse. Who was this man who'd just pulled a gun on me? He looked average enough with his paunchy belly and balding head, but I didn't trust him to let me explain what had happened. He was probably in league with Ingrid and Mrs. Garland.

The man stepped out of the French doors and onto the covered patio. "You're the only one here," he said. He stood about fifteen feet away, with a corner of the pool between us. "I've caught you red handed."

I backed away, my hands in the air again. "She needs help."

But he wasn't rushing forward to help her, nor was he reaching for his phone. He was sighting the gun on me. Nothing I could say or do could make this better. "Please call 911," I implored. Then, I did the only thing that made sense. I raced back through the gate, three shots ringing out behind me.

Two more shots fired out as I scrambled back up the flagstone pathway on the side of the house and past the sculpture in the front yard.

Clayton still stood at the door with the old woman, his hands over his ears. "What was that?"

"Let's go!" I shouted. "Fast!" I swung open the passenger side door and leapt inside, slamming the door behind me.

I locked the doors and ducked down in the car so no one could see me through the window.

At least a minute passed before Clayton unlocked his car and got in. "What was that all about?"

"That Ingrid woman was in the backyard. I knocked her out with a terracotta frog, and some guy shot at me."

Clayton laughed. "The lady at the door teaches acting lessons. She told me her students were rehearsing in the backyard. It sounds like you may have helped out in a murder scene." He pointed to his phone. "She showed me an article about her that was published in the paper."

"Can't you see this was a trap? It wasn't a peacock or acting class. My kidnappers wanted me to come here. They almost got me again. Now can we get out of here?" I begged. His car had a button for the ignition. I pressed it. Dang, it didn't work—his foot wasn't on the brake. "Please!"

"Whatever you say, Eva." He turned on the engine and pulled slowly away from the curb. "I love how you get so into these things, but it'd probably be best if you put on your seatbelt."

"Just drive," I said, hunkering down as close as I could get to the floor. "Is anyone following us?"

"No." I could tell from the strain in his voice that he still wanted to laugh. He cleared his throat and kept his eyes on the road.

After we'd driven about a mile, I felt safe enough to get back into my seat and put on my seatbelt. "I swear it was a real gun." We were still in the maze of streets around Mrs. Garland's house.

He gave the tiniest shrug. "Stage props have to look and sound real."

I shook my head. "It doesn't make sense that it was a rehearsal. They would have known I wasn't an actor."

"It's called ad-libbing." Clayton laughed again. Wade was totally wrong about us being soulmates.

I had to wonder again if this was real. It seemed strange that Clayton was so calm about it—just like Wade had been. "If you and Wade are playing a trick on me, it's time for it to end."

He glanced sideways at me for a second as he drove. "What do you mean?"

"You know what I mean. If you and Wade created this whole kidnapping scenario, it's gone too far." I placed my hand over the pain in my chest—probably from too much anxiety. "I'd like to go back to the warehouse and get my truck," I said. "I've had enough of Houston. I want to go home."

"Why would you think Wade and I created the kidnapping?" he said, sounding more serious. "I'm actually really interested in getting to the bottom of it all. Are you sure you don't want to go out and see the place where the trailer was?"

How could I put this so that he would understand? "Clayton! It's not fun to remember the things that have been happening to me."

"I know what will put your mind at ease." He pulled over to the side of the road. "I'm going to interview you about what just happened, so that if anyone accuses you of a crime, we'll have your story on record." He started videotaping me with his phone again.

How could he record me at a time like this? My thoughts were a tangle, and the pressure in my chest was about to smother me. Was I having a heart attack? "I'm not in the mood, Clayton."

He lowered the phone and pursed his lips. "You're right. It's probably better if we contact the police." He sounded more serious now, as if this was all really happening, and he was starting to believe me. "I think it'd be smart to tell them what happened."

"Are you sure they'll believe me? That man back at the house thought I was the one who attacked Ingrid, and I don't have any evidence to prove I didn't."

He tilted his head upward and nodded. "You could be right about that." His eyes widened. "Maybe you could hire a lawyer."

"With what money? I'm a student, working part-time."

"Look, Eva, I know you like to be independent, and I admire that about you, considering the family you come from."

It took a few moments until I could comprehend what he just said, but it still didn't make sense. "What do you mean, considering the family I come from?"

"Wade's told me about how successful your parents have been with their organic farms. You don't have to keep that a secret from me."

It was true my parents had a successful organic farm, but they also had ten children. They weren't exactly rolling in the dough, and it wasn't like Wade to brag about their success either. Clayton must have misunderstood something he said.

"I'm just trying to say that you aren't alone in this," Clayton said. "You have a great family, who can hire a great lawyer for you."

Visions of courtrooms and news stations danced through my head, but this time I couldn't imagine that any of this would bring me anything but bad publicity. My vlogging career would be over, and I could forget about my own fashion line.

Feeling a panic attack coming on, I drew in my breath. My parents always did say I was addicted to drama. "You heard the screams at that house, and don't tell me the sound of gunfire isn't still ringing in your ears. It wasn't my imagination. What I want to know is if you and Wade concocted all of it?"

"You think Wade and I have the time to do something like that?" he asked.

I'd had it with his indirect answers. All I wanted was to go home, curl up on my bed and sleep at least twelve hours. The only thing keeping me from doing that was the fact that my phone was still missing. "Look, Clayton, it's been really sweet of you to drive me around, but all I want right now is to get my phone back. Can I borrow your phone please to see if maybe Grant will answer this time?"

"You're not worried that this Grant might be one of the people who tried to kidnap you?"

"Not at all." I reached out my hand, but he didn't pass me his phone. "Why don't you want me to get my phone back?" I asked.

Only after rolling his eyes did he place his phone in my hand. "It's not that I don't want you to get your phone back. It's that I like spending time with you. Once you get your phone back, you'll have no reason to stay here."

Some women may have thought that was a sweet thing to say. I thought it was creepy. "I really should call now." I started punching my phone number into his phone.

"How about you call after we go to dinner?" he pled.

"I'd rather call now." The sooner I got away, the better. I listened as the phone on the other end rang. That was a good sign.

"If he doesn't answer, I'm taking you out to eat," Clayton said.

"I guess that'd be okay," I said, "but I plan to pay you back."

47

He whistled long and low. "It sure is different dating a rich girl."

My phone went to voicemail, so I hung up. "I'm not rich. I'd just prefer to have dinner without strings attached."

His brow fell, and I could tell he was processing what I'd just said. "I'm not that kind of guy."

"Good," I said, "because I'm not that kind of woman." I dialed my number on his phone again and waited.

On the fifth ring, a male voice answered. "Hello?" His tone was deep, yet hopeful.

Relief flooded through me. "Hi, this is Eva. Is this Grant?"

"Yeah, this is Grant!" Not only was I going to get my phone back and bring my horrible day in Houston to a close, I could see Grant again. "I'm so sorry I took your phone," he said. "I've been trying to get in touch with you."

I swallowed hard. I'd have to tell him later about how I lost his phone. "I'm sorry too."

"No. This is all my fault. I owe you big time. How about we meet for dinner tonight, and I can give you your phone?"

Dinner with Grant sounded perfect. "I'd love that." The only problem was that I'd just agreed to go to dinner with Clayton, who also happened to be my one and only ride. "But I already have plans for dinner." Likely Grant wouldn't feel too obligated to me once he learned what happened to his phone. That would be the end of all my hopes for getting to know Grant Tilney any better.

"How about a midafternoon snack then? We could meet at the café in a half hour or so if that works."

My stomach rumbled. It was two o'clock, and I hadn't eaten lunch. "That sounds great," I said, sneaking a glance toward Clayton, who wore a neutral expression on his face. I could still have dinner with him later, and I could get Dad's truck back after I got to the café.

It wasn't until after I hung up that I realized I'd have to ask Clayton to drop me off for my date with Grant. Super awkward.

"Do you think you could drop me off at that café?" I asked, forcing a happy tone into my voice as I gave him back his phone.

"You're not going to eat with him?"

"Just a little snack. I'm sure you heard that I'm still planning to go out to dinner with you later on."

His jaw pushed forward. "I was planning to spend the whole day with you." He sounded more disappointed than I would have expected. "I was already heading for this great Brazilian barbeque place."

He was already heading for the place he wanted to go to dinner? That's when it hit me. Clayton had the same definition for dinner that my grandmother had. I brought my hand to my forehead. "For you, dinner means the biggest meal of the day, not the last meal. I should have thought of that." I bit my lip. "Do you mind if we go to dinner later in the day—like supper? I promise I won't stuff myself at the café."

He huffed. "Whatever."

I wanted to say something like, "Way to be mature." Instead, I did the bigger thing. I considered that this guy was Wade's roommate and that, though I hadn't meant to, I'd stood him up for a date, and he had forgiven me for it. Not only that, he'd spent the morning driving me around. "You know what, why don't we imagine it's still yesterday, my kidnapping didn't happen, and we're just starting our drive to that escape room?" Maybe I'd misjudged Clayton, and he was a nicer guy than I thought. We'd just gotten started on the wrong foot with all my crazy kidnapping stuff. "I'd like to get to know you without all the distractions of my kidnapping."

"Okay," he said. "That sounds good."

"What are your hobbies?" I asked.

"Hobbies! I'm a student. I don't have time for hobbies."

Perhaps I wasn't going to like Clayton even when we started over. Oh, well. "Alright, you're a student. I get that. But what do you like to do for fun, other than go to escape rooms?"

"Movies and videogames." Clayton pulled away from the curb and started heading in what I hoped was the direction of the café.

"I like movies too. My favorite are the old black-and-whites, but Hitchcock movies are my favorites."

He shuddered as he came to a stop at a red light. "I can't stand Hitchcock, or anything black and white. The only old movie I like is *The Birds*. That one's a hoot."

I laughed. "A hoot! Good one." I paused, trying to read the expression on his face as his brows came together. Perhaps the pun had been accidental. I went on. "But *The Birds* is a Hitchcock movie. So is *Rear Window* and *North by Northwest*. Have you seen those?"

"No, I usually only watch stuff that's in color."

I was about to respond that both those movies were in color, but I thought better of it. Maybe he was thinking of another bird movie. "Wade said you're studying pre-med. What kind of medicine are you most interested in?"

"If it works out, I'd like to be a heart surgeon. They make good money."

It sounded like he was more into the idea of making money than the idea of helping people. This conversation was only convincing me to end our date sooner.

He turned to me, his face brightening. "If you want to hear something really interesting, I'll tell you how I got such a great deal on this Beemer."

This was a BMW? I hadn't noticed, and I didn't much care, but he was already going on with the story.

"There was this old guy in the neighborhood where I grew up who made a lot of money in oil. He bought himself a mansion with a five-car garage, but the guy was cheap. No gardener or maid for him. If he wanted someone to work for him, he'd hire a kid so he could pay less than minimum wage. I mean, we're talking a couple bucks an hour for hard labor. Most kids in the neighborhood wouldn't work for him. But I thought, what the hell, maybe if the old guy starts to lose his marbles as he ages, I can get more out of him. And you know what, that's exactly what happened. I worked for him from the time I was thirteen until I left for college. He got to where he couldn't remember my name or why I came over. He'd hand me my five bucks whether or not I mowed the lawn, and then we'd sit down and watch TV together. On my last visit before I left for college, I said to him, kind of joking, 'How about instead of that five bucks, you give me your black Beemer convertible?'"

"And he gave it to you?" Clayton's scruples were shocking enough, but how could the old man do something so ridiculous?

"He just said, 'Better you than my kids.' I had to help him find the keys and the title, but he was more than happy to let me have it."

I gulped. It sounded almost like elder abuse. "Have you gone back to see him since he gave you the car?"

He snorted as we pulled into the parking lot of the café. "Nope. I've been too busy with school."

If he was that busy with school, he didn't need to waste time taking me to dinner. "That reminds me, Clayton. I have an assignment I need to turn in tonight. I'm going to have to pass on dinner." It wasn't a lie. I did have an assignment … which was due next week. "Thank you so much for driving me around and helping me figure things out."

He parked in the same exact spot I'd parked the day before. "I thought you were on spring break. Why would your professor have an assignment due during your vacation?"

"The truth is, I'm a little behind on my classes, and I'm so tired from everything that's happened. Now that I have my purse, I can drive my truck home." I'd been so freaked out about the gun shots that I hadn't bothered to look in my purse for the keys. As I picked it up from the floor of Clayton's car, it felt heavier than normal. Opening it, I saw that it was filled with someone else's things—a tube of lipstick, sunglasses in a case, and some costume jewelry. I held up a ring with a gigantic blue stone.

51

CHAPTER 6

With the car parked at the diner, Clayton leaned toward me to look at the ring I'd found in my purse. "That's some cubic zirconium."

"It's not mine. I mean, this is my purse, but what's inside isn't mine. I think Ingrid must have been using my purse to carry her own things around. When I took it from her, I was hoping my things would be inside." Especially the keys to my truck. How was I going to get home now?

"Huh." Clayton had stopped the engine and was getting out of the car. He was coming into the diner with me. "I wonder if any of that jewelry is real."

That was just the sort of thing Wade would say if he was trying to fool me, which made me wonder once again if everything that had happened in the last twenty-four hours was a trick. But I couldn't think about that now. I had to do something to keep Clayton from coming into the diner with me. The last thing I wanted was for him to tag along on my date with Grant. I got out my door and spoke to him over the top of the car. "Umm. I know you're busy, Clayton, being pre-med and all. You don't have to wait around for me. I've got my truck back now. It's just down the street."

"I don't mind," he said as he turned to walk into the diner. "I'm sure Wade wouldn't want me to leave you alone with that guy after all that happened yesterday. Anyway, I'm hungry."

I stood my ground at the car. "I can handle myself, Clayton." I stuffed everything back inside the purse and shoved it under the front passenger seat. There was no use carrying it around if nothing inside was mine. Later on, after Clayton and I got back in the car, I'd figure out what to do with it.

When I looked up again, Clayton was holding the diner door open for me, waiting for me to go inside.

I groaned. "Would you mind protecting me from the other side of the restaurant? I didn't tell Grant you were coming."

"A lot of good I would be if I couldn't get to you in time."

Off to the side, I caught sight of Grant waving to me from a booth near the window. I waved back. I might need to ask him to help me get rid of Clayton. I locked Clayton's car door before closing it and walked toward the entrance.

Stepping into the café was like stepping back in time, and I don't just mean going back in time to a fifties-style diner. I mean that being there took away the tightness in my chest that I'd been feeling since the day before. I was looking forward to my future again instead of obsessing about all the bad things in the past.

The café was just as empty as when I first met Grant there. He was the only other customer. But there was the same smell of coffee, melted butter, hamburgers, and French fries. He stood as I approached and flashed me a smile that made me feel like Grace Kelly. Then he noticed Clayton beside me, and his eyes questioned mine.

"This is my brother's roommate, Clayton," I explained, touching Grant's forearm. I figured Grant would remember about my blind date.

They shook hands, and we slid into the booth, Clayton and I sitting opposite from Grant, who held my phone out for me. "Time for the exchange."

I bit my lip. This was what I'd been dreading. "I have a confession. I don't have your phone."

Grant leaned in. "That's okay."

He didn't seem too concerned, but I knew how upsetting losing a phone could be. "I'm so sorry. After I discovered we'd mixed up our phones, I tried to find you. The server told me you worked around the corner, so I went around the corner, knocked on the door of a warehouse, and asked the man who opened the door if you worked there." I explained everything in detail, as Grant kept his eyes on mine—how Ingrid and Ronald took away my purse and forced me into the car. It took a long time to go through it all, but I could tell from the crease in his forehead that he believed every word, and not only that, he wanted to help. Meanwhile Clayton fiddled with his phone.

When I was finished explaining, Grant shook his head and reached his hand for mine. "I'm sorry that happened to you. I feel responsible."

"It wasn't your fault," I said.

At this point, Clayton broke in, "If you need a new phone, I have a friend who's selling one he's barely used."

Grant didn't even break eye contact with me. "It sounds like you got caught in some kind of criminal operation."

"I guess it could have had something to do with drugs or human trafficking, but it seemed more like a really bad murder mystery." I thought of Ingrid. "I just hope there wasn't a murder."

Clayton's phone rang. He answered it, but he kept having to repeat himself and then excused himself to go outside, where the reception was better.

"Think maybe he feels threatened that I asked you out to eat?" Grant asked as we watched Clayton walk away from the table.

I giggled. "Oh, you don't have to buy me anything. I mean, I already lost your phone."

"But I want to buy you lunch. You will let me, won't you?"

I felt a blush creep over my cheeks. "Of course, I'll let you. But I already owe you for the phone."

"Oh, forget about the phone. It's nothing compared to what I've put you through."

"Do you believe me about the kidnapping?"

His eyes narrowed and he leaned in closer, as if he were about to tell me a secret. "Absolutely."

"I'm still sorry I took your phone. How can I make it up to you?" He traced the edge of my menu with his finger. "All I want is a half hour of your time, and our friend Clayton has already stolen a good five minutes of it."

"He probably didn't see it as stealing."

He winked. "Well, he should have. It's an accepted fact in the male world that when you ask a woman to lunch, another male should not tag along. A lunch date is a sacred contract between a man and woman."

"You make it sound like marriage or something." There I went again, speaking before I thought things through. My cheeks were probably flaming red.

He chuckled. Good thing he didn't take me too seriously. "I wouldn't go that far, but in some ways, it's similar. We've entered into an agreement that we'll spend the next half hour with each other. You won't be distracted by other men. I won't be distracted by other women."

"If that's all it includes, I can keep my end of the bargain," I said.

He reached out, now tracing the tip of his finger over the top of my hand. "Well, there is a little more. We must put up with each other through sickness and health. For better or for worse. Until dessert do we part."

"Until dessert do we part," I repeated.

At that point, our server came to take our orders, and Grant took his hand away. Though I hadn't even bothered to look at the menu, I knew exactly what I wanted—a bacon cheeseburger with onion rings. Stress always brought out my need for calories.

After she left, he leaned toward me, lowering his voice. "Since we're making confessions," he said. "I have to confess that if it hadn't been for all the trouble I caused you, I wouldn't have any regrets at all about switching phones. I was hoping I'd get to see you again."

"Me too," I said. "There's so much more I wanted to talk to you about. I didn't even get a chance to ask what you do for work."

For the first time, his eyes darted toward the window. "My work isn't interesting."

"The server told me you work for your family and that you drive a truck."

His gaze returned to mine. "You don't seem the type to be interested in truck driving."

He had me there. I didn't care about truck drivers before I met him. "Well, I'm interested now."

"You already know all there is to know. I work for my family, and I drive a truck." He shrugged, and I wondered if he

55

thought I was too nosy. Maybe he was more of the private type than he seemed. "What do you do for work?" he asked.

"I help with my family's orchard. We raise organic pecans and peaches."

He grinned, creating a dimple in one cheek. "I can just see you climbing a peach tree in one of your Grace Kelly get-ups."

"I usually wear jeans and a T-shirt, but if you ever come to visit, I'll dress up."

His eyes opened wide. He had the most gorgeous dark blue eyes. "Then I'm definitely coming. I can bake you a pie when we're all done."

"Good," I said, "because I can't bake pies to save my life. Neither can anyone else in my family. At Thanksgiving, we get our pies frozen from the grocery store."

He laughed. "That's the saddest thing I've ever heard."

"Isn't it? I can cook, though. I make delicious lasagna, chili, Coq Au Vin, anything at all really. Just don't ask me to bake cupcakes."

"Tell you what, next time we get together, you can cook dinner. I'll make dessert."

"Deal!"

No sooner had I said it than I heard a knock at the window beside me and turned to see Clayton, motioning for me to come outside. I shook my head. I had, after all, promised to ignore every other man except Grant for the next half hour.

But as soon as I turned back to Grant, Clayton knocked again, this time harder. "Now," he mouthed.

"I'm starting to lose patience with him," Grant said through a tight smile.

"Me too." I put my hand up to the side of my face, blocking my view of Clayton.

Clayton wasn't ready to be ignored, though. He rushed inside the diner and plopped down on the seat beside me. "That was the police on the phone. They got my number from that old lady I talked to at Mrs. Garland's house. They said you're a possible suspect. I checked to make sure the call was legit and found this on the news." He slid his phone onto the table in front of me. There, right on the news website was video footage of me hitting Ingrid over the head and then taking her purse.

My worries returned in a rush, so much stronger than I'd felt them before. There must have been a security camera somewhere at the back of that house. Scrolling down through the article, I couldn't help reading the words "armed robbery" out loud.

"I told the police that you're here," he said, "I thought it was the right thing to cooperate."

I continued to stare at the news article. "I wasn't armed … unless they consider a terra cotta frog an arm. I was only trying to protect myself. I didn't steal anything either. All I did was take back my purse." Would the police believe me if I talked to them again? I didn't have any proof that Ingrid had been the one who kidnapped me, or that she had taken my purse. I didn't even have proof that the red clutch purse had once been mine.

"I just remembered," Clayton said, getting up from his seat, "I have somewhere I need to be."

Grant's forehead crinkled with concern. "But aren't you a witness too?" he called after Clayton. "Shouldn't you talk to the police together?"

Out the window, we watched Clayton get into his car and pull out of the parking lot. So much for his help. I didn't blame him, of course. I wouldn't have wanted to keep helping me either. It was probably the sort of thing that you could go to jail for.

I leaned closer to Grant, keeping my voice low. "I talked to the police yesterday, but it was like someone was trying to frame me. I couldn't prove anything I said. The car I drove didn't belong to the people who kidnapped me—it was stolen—and when I took the officer back to the trailer where the kidnappers tried to kill me, there was an old man there who said I'd been heckling him. Today has been the same way. The janitor at the warehouse gave us an address where I could find the owner. When we got to the house, I heard someone scream, and when I went to find out if anyone needed help, Ingrid was standing there, laughing at me. I thought she was going to kidnap me again, so I hit her over the head. Then I took the purse she was carrying, which was the purse she took

57

from me yesterday. I guess that's why they're saying I robbed her."
I looked at Grant as he sat there, shaking his head. There was something in the set of his jaw, as if anger brewed just below the surface. "Sometimes I wonder if this is all a trick my brother is pulling on me. You would tell me if you knew it was a trick, wouldn't you?"

He turned to look out the window. "It's not a trick."

A car was pulling into the parking lot, and as soon as I saw who was inside, I ducked below the window. It was Ronald and that old man from the trailer. "That's the man that kidnapped me," I whispered, my voice shaking, "and the other one is the man from the trailer." I slipped down under the table, crouching on the tile floor beside Grant's feet. "What are they doing?"

He swiveled his knees to cover me from the front of the table. "They're coming inside."

Clayton had said the police had called him and were coming to talk to me. Now, instead of the police, these two showed up. What were the odds that it was the bad guys, not the police, who'd called Clayton? I was guessing around ninety-nine-point-nine percent. "They must know I'm here. I need a place to hide." I wished I had my truck parked here instead of at the warehouse. "How far are they from the door? Do I have time to run to the restroom?" Then I caught sight of Grant's keys, lying on the seat beside him. "Or out to your truck? Do I have time to hide in your truck?"

"If you hurry." He handed me his keys, pointing out the square-shaped, silver one. "It's the big rig on the other side of the building. Go out the back exit." He pointed to a door past the restrooms. "Hurry."

He did believe me, and not only that, he was helping me. I hunkered down below the windows. Keeping myself bent over, I ran toward the back door. Then I thought of how Grant could get in trouble for this.

I turned back to him. "Are you sure?" I mouthed.

He tilted his head toward the exit. "Go," he said.

There was no time to discuss it any more. If I was going to run, I had to run now.

I opened the door an inch and peeked outside. Grant's big rig stood ten feet in front of me. It was just the truck cab—detached from the semi-trailer.

I ran to it, climbed up on the side rail and slid the key into the lock. The door was bigger and heavier than the doors I was used to, but I pulled it open. At the front of the truck were two big seats, much like the seats in my parents' minivan, only bigger with a wide space between them. I shut the door behind me, squeezed past the steering wheel, and crouched down to the floor. It was probably hot enough in there to kill a dog, but I didn't dare crack open a window—Ronald and that other guy might notice. I could stand the heat for a few minutes. I crawled behind the front seats. There was a living space back there with a tiny microwave, fridge and two bunks along the back wall. The bottom bunk was made with a sheet and blanket on it. The top bunk was empty.

I rested my back against the back of the driver's seat, wondering how long I'd have to sit here in the heat, surveying the contents of the shelves. In the storage compartment beside the bed, I saw a few water bottles, a jacket, a carry-on suitcase, and a few books. One was a travel book about South America. Another was fiction and looked like a spy novel.

I should have been stressing about the fact that the police suspected me of armed robbery. Instead, I was wondering what Grant kept in the refrigerator or in the other little cabinets around the bed. It would have been rude to open any of them. I'd learned my lesson about nosing around when I'd gone to that warehouse and found the Leslie Kaplan note.

To take my mind off the heat, I reached for the South American travel book. I'd always wanted to go to Manchu Pichu in Peru and maybe to some of the Aztec ruins in Mexico. It looked like Grant did too. He had about twenty different locations flagged with sticky notes. I paged through each one. He did seem to have an interest in archaeological settings, but he seemed more interested in rainforests, even in what I considered the more dangerous locations—Columbia, Venezuela, Nicaragua. Was he one of those adrenaline addicts?

Then I remembered I had something more important to do. I picked up my phone, noticing that it was fully charged. Grant must have kept it plugged in. I typed in the name Leslie Kaplan. Dozens of photographs, all of different people, covered the screen. None of them lived in Texas.

What was I doing? If the bad guys knew I was at the café, they could easily figure out I'd hidden in Grant's truck. Now, not only had I gotten myself in trouble. I'd gotten him in trouble too.

I heard the door open. "Don't say anything," Grant muttered as he sat down in his seat. He placed a paper bag of take-out on the floor beside me, the scent of bacon cheeseburgers and onion rings wafting through the truck's cabin. He bent to put on his seat belt. "They're watching."

Staying seated on the floor with my knees pulled up to my chest, I handed the keys to him, and he started the truck. The air conditioning came on with a whoosh. Thank goodness! The stereo came on next, playing a jazzy classic that sounded like Gershwin, which wasn't what I would have expected at all. Then again, Grant was the classy type. He just kept surprising me. I liked that about him.

I closed the book and slipped it back on the shelf as the truck started moving forward. Once we got out of the parking lot, he spoke again. "Those guys asked if I'd seen you. I told them you left five minutes before they got there."

"Thank you." I let my breathing slow, resting my back against the air conditioning vent. "I hope they don't suspect you of anything."

"If they do, I can handle it."

"You can drop me off wherever people won't notice me much. I can take public transportation from there."

"That wouldn't be very gentlemanly of me. Besides, we finally got rid of that Clayton guy. I feel like we should take advantage of that and spend our thirty minutes together. Let's just think of this as an extension of our lunch date."

As much as I didn't want him to get involved, I couldn't resist spending a few more minutes with him. Not only did I like him, Grant had a level-headed steadiness about him that might be the one thing to get me through this without a nervous breakdown. I could talk to the police later—after I figured out how to prove that I was telling the truth.

CHAPTER 7

Not only was it my first time inside the cab of a truck, I was also neglecting to wear my seatbelt again. My parents had always been sticklers for seatbelts. But right now, it was safer to be where Ronald and the old man from the trailer couldn't see me. For all I knew, they could be following us in their car. Still, I felt safe within the shelter of Grant's truck.

Sitting on the floor behind Grant's seat, I smelled the cheeseburger and onion rings that were also in front of me. "Sorry it took me so long," he said, after we'd left the diner's parking lot. "I promised I'd give you lunch, and I wanted to make sure you got what you ordered."

Just as I was reaching for the bag, he spoke again, "But, remember our deal. We're eating lunch together. There's a parking lot a few streets away where I can park while we eat."

His casual tone put me at ease, making me feel as if this were a date instead of a run for my life. "Parking with a man," I said, drawing out my syllables. "My mother wouldn't approve." Especially not since this cab was a rolling bedroom.

"My father would be fine with it," he said, "Parking with an armed robbery suspect, though. He might take issue with that."

"Come on! You know it was my kidnappers who called Clayton, not the police. I'm not a criminal." I reached for the bag again. "But if it'll put your mind at ease, we can eat while you drive me to the police station."

He pulled it away from me. "Oh, no, you don't. We're going to have a leisurely lunch with the truck parked. I'll promise not to do anything I wouldn't do if your mother were here, and you'll promise not to hit me over the head and rob me. Deal?"

That was easy for him to say. He didn't know my mother's ultra-conservative standards. I wasn't even supposed to kiss a man unless I was engaged to him. "My mother is a very conservative, Christian woman, so when you say you won't do anything she wouldn't approve of …"

He held one hand up off the steering wheel, as if he were taking an oath. "You're safe with me. I won't touch you as long as we're in the truck."

"Good."

"But," he said, "you're free to touch me all you want."

"That sounds good." There I was again, letting my heart speak before my head thought things through.

He laughed. "I'm glad you think so. For an armed robbery suspect, you're pretty entertaining."

Funny how he could joke about me being a criminal when he hardly knew me. He had no reason to trust me. "What if it really was the police who called Clayton, and I really am a dangerous criminal? It's probably not the best idea for you to be driving me around."

He checked his rearview mirror before making a left-hand turn. "Well, I've watched all the seasons of my favorite television shows, and there aren't any good games on, so meeting up with a criminal is just about the best thing that could have happened today."

I laughed. It felt good to have someone believe me, even better that he was handsome and funny. "You must really believe my crazy story."

"I do." He stopped the truck, and flipped a switch to turn on the auxiliary air conditioners. "Here we are at the parking lot. Time for lunch." He swiveled his seat around and opened a little cabinet above me. From it, he pulled out two paper plates, two paper cups, and some plastic utensils.

He was such a gentleman, it was almost too good to be true. But I couldn't let myself worry that Grant was anything other than a good guy. Sure, it could've been his good looks or his charisma that swayed me, but I wanted to believe it was more than that—I could sense his inner goodness, and that's why I ignored all my parents' warnings about strange men. Of course, it had been my idea to hide out in his truck. I'd asked for his help, and he'd agreed to it. "Seriously, though," I asked, "why are you risking yourself for me?"

"Because you're innocent."

I watched as he removed two paper-wrapped burgers from the bag. "Yesterday, the police couldn't find any evidence to support what I told them," I said, "but I have more ways to prove my story today. Clayton was with me before I saw Ingrid in that backyard. He heard the screaming."

"Were there any other witnesses—other than Clayton?" The hesitation in his voice told me he didn't have much confidence that Clayton would help defend me.

How could I prove my innocence then? All the other witnesses seemed to be in league with my kidnappers. I had to come up with some better evidence to prove my case. "I guess I'd better do some more investigating on my own before I talk to the police."

Grant's face was a study in concentration. He was looking at me, but his mind seemed to be elsewhere.

Was he worried about getting involved? "You don't need to help me with that part," I said. "I'm just grateful you helped me get out of the diner."

He straightened up and pressed his lips into a smile. "But I want to help you."

I breathed a sigh of relief. I hadn't known it, but I'd been hoping he'd say that. "I promise I'm innocent."

"Then there's nothing for me to worry about." He spread a blanket on the floor of the truck cab, sat down, and handed me the take-out bag.

There was, on the other hand, plenty for me to worry about. The police suspected me of armed robbery, I'd been kidnapped, and videos of me hitting Ingrid over the head were going viral.

If it weren't for Grant, my anxiety would have paralyzed me. Instead, I was sitting here, eating a picnic in a truck cab. It felt like an adventure. I reflected again on how it all started the day before in the diner while I was waiting for Wade to show up. He had promised to take me to an escape room, and, once again, I wondered if this whole experience was one of Wade's tricks. He was a prankster, after all, and he knew I loved a good mystery. Sure, I wasn't inside an escape room, but could it be that Wade was behind this whole mystery? It didn't seem likely—given that a woman tried to poison me and that I'd talked to an actual policeman—but I had to make sure, once and for all, that Grant wasn't just acting a role in a prank.

If Grant was Wade's friend, I needed to get him to slip up and say so. Maybe if I casually mentioned something about Wade, I could get Grant to come out of character. Then I would know this whole thing was a charade. "Did Wade ever tell you about our dog named Ruffles?" Wade was always talking about that dog.

"Who's Wade?" he asked before biting into his burger.

"My brother."

He took his time chewing and swallowing. "I've never met your brother."

So much for that attempt. "Someone else put you up to this?"

His eyebrows knit together. "Put me up to what?"

"Walking into the diner, saying I looked like Grace Kelly, switching phones with me."

"You did look like Grace Kelly in that dress."

"But did someone ask you to talk to me yesterday at the diner?"

He dipped his onion ring in ketchup as if nothing I could say would faze him. "No."

"Promise?"

"I promise."

"Huh." I guessed I had to trust him and accept the fact that everything I'd experienced had been real. I really had been kidnapped. Someone really had tried to kill me. And worst of all, someone had accused me of a heinous crime.

That meant I needed to try even harder to prove my innocence. I needed to get back to my investigation. And I could start with the one thing I'd been wondering since the very beginning. "Have you ever heard of Leslie Kaplan?" I asked. Since he worked near the warehouse where I'd been kidnapped, it was possible he knew something about her.

He wagged his finger back and forth. "No investigating while we eat. It's bad for your digestion."

I reached for an onion ring. Though I knew he was right about me needing to relax, I couldn't help goading him. "You sure do have a lot of rules when it comes to eating lunch."

He opened the mini fridge beside him and pulled out a couple bottles of water. "It's the best way I know to lead a peaceful existence."

I tried to imagine what his peaceful existence consisted of, but I still knew so little about him. "What do you like to do in your free time, other than make up rules, bake pies, and watch TV?"

"I'm a pretty boring guy, but I like to toss a baseball around."

Baseball. He did seem like the boy-next-door type. "We should play together sometime," I said. "How about fishing? Yes or no?"

"A definite yes."

"Me too." I bit into my onion ring and closed my eyes to appreciate its savor. Aside from all my problems, could this moment be any more perfect? He liked fishing, baseball, and old movies. I decided to go out on a limb and ask the question that always separated the real men from the boys. "How do you feel about women scientists?" He was, after all, a truck driver, and even other guys who went to college with me could become a little distant once they found out I was studying forensic science.

"I'd say good for you."

It was the perfect answer, so perfect, in fact, that I had to take my questioning a step further. "Have you ever gone to college?"

He nodded as he chewed his burger. Unlike my brothers, he waited until he'd swallowed to answer. "I have a Juris Doctorate."

I couldn't have been more shocked—he was a truck driver with a law degree. Did those actually exist? I did need a lawyer, though, and it also helped me understand his reaction when I said Clayton wouldn't make a good witness. The last two days may have been the unluckiest of my life, but at least providence had tipped the scales a little. I had a lawyer to help me plan my defense. "You're really a lawyer?"

"Yes. I've just taken some time off to help with the family business." His mouth stayed neutral, but his eye brows dropped.

They must have big trouble with the family business to make Grant want to leave his practice—perhaps a bankruptcy. "Your family must appreciate that."

He shrugged and huffed out a laugh. "That's debatable."

"What kind of law did you practice?"

"Estate planning."

"I don't suppose that'll be any help for me in these circumstances."

"No, but I'm well versed in Perry Mason. Does that put your mind at ease?"

I laughed. "Definitely." I bit into my cheeseburger and savored another bite of diner goodness.

We settled into a comfortable silence. A flutter of pleasure danced through me as I glanced at Grant. It had never been so easy to talk to a guy, and having four brothers, I considered myself an expert on male communication. On every other date I'd been on, there were awkward pauses and misinterpreted phrases, but Grant understood everything I said just as I meant it, and even when we weren't talking, I felt perfectly comfortable.

Plus, he was easy on the eyes.

When I spoke again, there were only a few crumbs left on our paper plates. "Are you sure you have time to help me?" I said, wiping my face with a napkin. "Don't you have a trucking schedule to keep?"

He shook his head. "I told you you're stuck with me until after dessert, and that might be a while. I'm way too full to have anything else right now."

I should have asked him again about Leslie Kaplan since we were finished eating, but the food had relaxed me too much. I had to know more about Grant before we started talking again about my problems. "Would it be rude of me to ask how old you are?"

"Twenty-eight. Is that too old?"

That made him the oldest guy I'd ever dated, but an eight-year age gap wasn't too much. At least I didn't think so. "It's just right," I said, repeating a line from *It's a Wonderful Life*. "Your age fits you."

"Good one," he said, "but you should really do it this way." He cleared his throat. "Oh, no, no," he said, sounding just like Jimmy Stewart. "Just right. Your age fits you."

"Very impressive," I said, putting an extra emphasis on impress, so he'd catch my pun. I'd always liked men who could do impressions.

"I suppose it would be rude to ask how old you are," he said.

"Extremely rude. I'll be twenty-one next week."

He gave a slight nod, as if he'd expected me to say twenty-one, which I guessed meant he was okay with the age gap.

"Where exactly are we?" I asked, rising up on my knees to look out the window.

Grant pulled me back down. "I didn't want to tell you this, but a car followed us here."

"Why did you park then?"

"I didn't want to look suspicious. Now, if you don't mind sitting still for a while, I'm going to take the trash out." He stuffed all our trash back into the take-out bag, and stood up. "See you in a minute."

A car had followed us? It had to be the one Ronald was driving. He knew I was here. The sooner I could prove my innocence and get my kidnappers behind bars, the better. I needed to get back to my investigation, and first on my list was Leslie Kaplan. If I could find out who she was and maybe talk to her, perhaps she could help me explain this whole situation to the police. I pulled my phone back out of my pocket and put her name into a search engine again. For someone so elusive to my kidnappers, she was surprisingly easy to find. I found her address in Houston, as well as a phone number, an e-mail address, and several social media accounts. Without hesitating, I called the phone number—I wouldn't have a chance if they threw me in jail later. No one answered, and the voicemail box wasn't set up, so I sent her a text, asking her to call me.

Putting her address into my search box, I saw that she lived in a little bungalow in the heart of the city, just the type of place that would have been featured in fifties sitcoms. It had a tiny front porch with enough space for a couple of red rocking chairs. A rose garden ran under the porch railings, and baskets of impatiens hung from the eaves. Best of all, the front door was Dutch style and split in a horizontal line across the middle. In short, it was my dream house, which meant that Leslie Kaplan couldn't be all bad. She probably watched old movies and shopped at thrift stores. I had to get to her house.

As I found directions to the house, the truck door opened, and Grant said, "Yes, sir," in the most casual tone. At first, I thought he was calling me sir. Then he spoke again, and I realized he was speaking to someone outside the truck. "Like I said, you're free to look inside if you'd like."

Someone was about to come inside the truck. Whoever it was—Ronald, a policeman, or someone else—was no doubt looking for me.

I had to hide fast.

CHAPTER 8

What was Grant thinking to let someone search his truck? My eyes darted from one side of the truck cab to the other. There wasn't a closet or cabinet large enough to hold me. If I lay on one of the bunks, they would see me right away.

I grabbed the blanket Grant had used for our picnic. I'd just have to hope there was room enough for me under the bed, where Grant kept his suitcases. Trying not to make a sound, I pulled them out. Then I squished my body into the small space under the bottom bunk. It was much narrower than the bed, and I guessed that was probably because I was in between two wheel wells, but I wedged most of my body into the space. The only problem was that my legs didn't fit, but there was no time to find another hiding spot. I could hear Grant climbing up into the truck already. "Come on up," he said.

All I had time to do was to throw the blanket over my legs. Then I waited for the inevitable. Surely, this wouldn't fool anyone.

Why was I doing this anyway? I was innocent. I should have just called the police. At least, then I could be safe from Ronald and company.

It was too late now, though. Grant had already lied for me. I had to do my best to keep him safe.

"This is one of the nicer cabs," someone said. She wasn't a man like I'd expected. She had a delicate, female timbre.

"What did that blonde say to you at the diner?" another voice asked. This one was a male, but he didn't sound like Ronald.

"Not much," Grant answered. He didn't sound at all nervous. In fact, though I couldn't see his face, I could have sworn he was smiling. "I just happened to find her phone and wanted to give it back to her."

Footsteps approached me. I shut my eyes tight and held my breath until bam—something hard slammed into my toe. It was the kind of bone-crushing pain that normally would have sent me hopping out of the truck, shouting curses my mother would barely approve.

Instead, I bit the inside of my cheek until it bled.

"Sorry about the mess," Grant said, shoving another object into my shin. "If I'd known I was going to have guests, I would have straightened up these suitcases before you got here."

"No worries," the woman responded. "We just wanted to check—because of what that waitress at the diner said."

"No problem," Grant said. "Anything I can do to help?"

And that is when my phone, which was in my pocket, decided to sing "You're So Vain" by Carly Simon. It was Wade's ringtone.

The conversation paused. "Do you need to get that?" the man asked.

"Oh, that's my ex calling," Grant said. "Third time today. Some people just don't know when to stop."

The thought distracted me, for just a moment, from the issues at hand. I wondered if Grant really had an ex and, if so, whether she was an ex-wife or girlfriend.

"You have a special ringtone for your ex?" The woman asked.

Grant laughed. "Yes. I'm sure you don't have time to hear the whole story about it."

"We've got plenty—" the woman began to say, but the man interrupted.

"We'd better get going," he said. "Come on, Denise."

I listened as they stepped outside the door and climbed down the side of the truck.

Grant shut the door and turned on the engine. Then we began moving.

He didn't speak for another five minutes and when he finally did say something, it wasn't at all what I was expecting. "How'd you like to take a trip up North?"

I kicked the suitcases out from in front of me, threw off the blanket, and wriggled out from my hiding spot. "Who were those people?"

"One was the same guy who was in the parking lot in the diner. Only this time, he had a woman with him."

"So they weren't the police—and you let them search the truck anyway?"

He shrugged. "I figured if they thought you weren't here, it'd throw them off our track."

I'd thought that Mrs. Garland only had Ingrid, Ronald, and the guy from the trailer on her team. Now there was this Denise person to add to the mix. Could it be that she had a whole army of bad guys, and they were all out looking for me?

"Now how about that trip up North?" Grant said.

Why was he in such a hurry to take me up North, rather than talk to the police?

"All I want to do is visit Leslie Kaplan's house—it's the one last bit of evidence I need before I turn myself into the police." He was stopped at a light, so I passed him my phone, on which I'd pulled up the directions to her idyllic street. "Her house isn't all that far away."

He held his jaw tight, and, for the first time, it seemed like I was stressing him out. He shook his head. "I'm not sure you appreciate how much danger you're in."

I crawled closer, so I was sitting on the floor beside his seat. "Of course I do. I've been living it for the past twenty-four hours. That's why I need to find out about this Leslie Kaplan. She's the one who can help me understand everything. Can we please go to her house?" I took my phone back from him.

"Trust me, Eva. That's not a good idea." A car behind us honked, and Grant let his foot off the brake to go through the intersection.

"How would you know what's a good idea and what's not? You haven't been around these people who kidnapped me." I spotted a baseball cap I hadn't noticed before on the little shelf with Grant's books. "If you'll let me borrow your baseball cap and maybe some of your clothes, I can work out a disguise. Then maybe the bad guys won't recognize me."

"Good idea," he said. "How long are you planning to spend at Leslie Kaplan's house?"

"That depends on whether she's home when we get there. We might have to wait around a while."

72

He huffed out a laugh. Then he recovered and became serious. "How about we stay long enough for you to leave her a note? I don't have any more time than that. I'm supposed to hook up to my semi-trailer in an hour."

I had been hoping for more, but this way I had at least a chance of meeting Leslie. "I guess it'll have to do." I looked back at my phone. "Do you want my phone to give you directions?"

He was already changing lanes. "I know how to get there. Go ahead and change your clothes. You're welcome to anything you find in my suitcase."

He trusted me to look through his bags? It felt a little intimate. "I'm not sure I'm ready for that kind of commitment. I know we had lunch together and all. It's just that—"

"There's nothing in my suitcase that will embarrass you. I promise."

I crawled back to the little bedroom space and turned the suitcase right-side-up. It was one of those carry-on types, so as I unzipped it, I wasn't expecting to find much inside. Sure enough, there were only a few T-shirts, one pair of jeans, and a pair of pajama pants, as well as some boxer shorts. I picked the most nondescript of the T-shirts—a dark blue, plain one. It was about four sizes too big, which wasn't a problem. I could wear it like a tunic. I just needed something to cinch it around my waist. "Do you have a belt in here?"

"Check the outside pocket."

I unzipped the side pocket and reached inside. Sure enough, I found a belt, but I also found a phone. It was Grant's phone—the same phone I'd lost at the warehouse. It had the same scratch across the back of the case and the same little bubble on the screen protector.

He'd been lying to me.

CHAPTER 9

The fact that Grant had my phone meant one of two possibilities. The first was that he was one of the bad guys. The second was that he was one of Wade's friends, playing an elaborate hoax on me, and setting me up with Grant at the same time.

Preferring the second explanation, I picked up my own phone and called Wade. As grateful as I was to have gotten to know Grant, the game had gone on long enough. I was ready to return to my low-stress reality.

"Eva," Wade answered, his voice breathless and his volume low. He was a much better actor than I'd ever realized. "Are you okay?"

My voice came out husky and low, as if I were the heroine in a film noire. "The jig is up, Wade. I know you're behind all of it." I was still sitting on the floor in the back of the truck cab.

"What do you mean I'm behind all of it? I don't even know what's going on. Look, I'm here talking to the police at the station, and I think the best thing for you to do is to turn yourself in. I can come get you if it'll make you more comfortable."

He was still playing the game, which was just like him. He never did know when to be serious, but I'd had enough. "I told you I'm onto you, Wade. I know it's all been a trick, and I've gotta hand it to you! It has been really impressive. Your friends are such great actors. Not to mention those police officers out in the country."

"Eva!" He growled my name, the way he did when he was super frustrated. "It wasn't a scheme. You've got yourself mixed up in a huge mess, and we need to sort it out."

His tone sent a chill down my spine. Maybe this was real after all, and I'd willingly placed myself in the bad guy's vehicle— with no easy way to escape. Suddenly, that cheeseburger wasn't sitting at all right on my stomach. How was I going to keep my cool without letting Grant know I was onto him?

But then I remembered next week was my twenty-first birthday. Had Wade planned a surprise birthday party? I'd thrown one for him when he turned twenty-one. That's probably what all this was about. I pictured a group of my friends gathered in the middle of a fake police station. They would have a huge birthday cake set up on a card table. Probably everyone in my family was there now, waiting for me. "Okay," I said. "That sounds fun."

He heaved a sigh. "Incorrigible." Wade had always loved using big words to describe me, as if I wouldn't know what they meant.

I huffed and clicked the end call button. Leave it to Wade to celebrate my birthday in the most annoying way ever. This whole thing had gone on long enough.

Within a few seconds, my phone rang. I looked at the caller ID. "It's Wade again," I told Grant. "I'm not going to answer it."

"Eva," Grant said from the front seat, "I need you to listen carefully. This isn't a game. You really are in trouble, but not in the way Wade thinks."

His gravelly tone made my stomach cramp return. What did he mean that I wasn't in trouble the way Wade thought? What could be worse than being accused of a crime? "If you're trying to freak me out, it's working." I stared down at my phone as Wade's call went to voicemail.

The muscles in Grant's neck tensed, and he raked his hand through his hair. "I'm not trying to freak you out. I'm trying to protect you. You've gotten yourself mixed up with some very dangerous people." He turned briefly toward me, but he gave no smile or wink to hint that he was joking.

I wrapped my arms around myself, rocking back and forth. Mrs. Garland, Ingrid, and Ronald weren't just actors. They were really after me. Maybe Wade was right. "I should talk to the police then."

He shook his head. "Normally, that would be the right choice." He heaved a sigh. "But not in this case." He sounded like he knew all about this case.

"And you know this how?" I asked as I crawled across the floor of the truck cab until I could see the side of Grant's face. He turned toward me, flashing me the saddest smile I'd ever seen. "I've already said more than I should ... for your safety."

How could Grant know so much about the bad guys without actually being one himself? Any normal person would have taken me to the police.

My throat tightened. What if Grant didn't really like me? What if he'd been play-acting everything, pretending to be a perfect match for me? Maybe he didn't like old movies as much as I did, and he'd only said he was okay with female scientists because he wanted me to trust him.

I gulped. "Maybe you should drop me off somewhere."

He took his time answering. "I will if you really want me to ... It's your choice ... but it's not a good idea for you to be alone right now."

I'd heard before that women needed to trust their gut in situations like these. I wasn't quite sure what that meant, but I did know that I was the one who tried to find Grant's place of employment, and I was the one who got into this truck. He hadn't forced me into this situation—I'd asked him to help me.

"My dad has a house in Oklahoma," he said. "While I was waiting for our food at the restaurant, I called him to ask if we could stay the night."

Oklahoma? It was at least six hours just to the border. I had to consider the situation once again. Was Grant really someone I could trust? "I found your phone in your backpack. You never told me that you got it back."

"Right." His neck turned red. "Like I said, it's better if you don't know."

Did kidnappers get embarrassed like that? It made me want to believe that he really was lying to protect me, but how could a lie protect me? If I knew the truth, I could protect myself. "It'd be easier to trust you if I knew how you got your phone back," I said. As it was, it seemed like he was one of the bad guys.

"I don't blame you for not trusting me." He paused. "But I'm telling the truth."

"Well, I can't just go to Oklahoma with you because you're hot."

His head whipped toward me as soon as I said the word hot, and a grin flashed across his face. My mom had always told me not to use that word—hot—to describe a man, and now I could see why. I'd definitely gratified his ego. Not that he didn't deserve some praise. It just wasn't my aim at the moment.

He pressed his lips into an exaggerated frown. "I have a brain, you know."

I could tell that he was teasing me, but I played along anyway. "I'm just saying that I need more from your brain, specifically the things you're trying to hide from me. That's how you gain my trust—tell me your secrets."

"Okay ... how about if I tell you that I think you're very attractive."

It wasn't the kind of secret I was hoping for, but how could I resist taking that bait? "And how about my brain?"

"The inside part of you is what attracts me the most."

His expression remained serious, but his words—the inside part of him—demanded a reaction. "Oh, that's not creepy at all."

He was changing lanes now, as relaxed as ever. "What I meant was that I like your personality. Most women I know have become hardened and cynical, but you assume that most people are good."

"My brothers would say I'm naïve."

"No. A better word is idealistic. I like that about you."

I folded my arms, still aware that he hadn't revealed anything I really wanted to know. "Which is why you think I'll trust you without your having to provide believable details about your involvement in this mess?"

"I'm trying to pay you a compliment."

"Thank you for your compliment." I tried to sound sincere, though I couldn't help that a sarcastic tone may have slipped through. "I would really like to know how you're involved in this whole Leslie Kaplan thing. Do you know Ingrid and Ronald? They work near you."

As usual, I had to wait for his answer. "I know all of them—Ronald, Ingrid, and the one you call Mrs. Garland," he said, speaking just above a whisper. "They're dangerous people."

77

I couldn't help crawling to the front of the truck and checking the truck's mirrors to make sure Ingrid and Ronald weren't following us, but the coast seemed clear. It was so strange that he could know so much about them without being on their side. If he wasn't one of them, he should have known nothing about them. Wasn't that they way it worked? Every time I saw a news crew interview a criminal's neighbors, the neighbors knew nothing about the criminal. If Grant wasn't involved with Ingrid and Ronald, he would probably tell me that they were nice, quiet people. The fact that he knew they were bad had to mean he was in on the crime. "How do I know you're not a dangerous person?"

"Some people think I am." His words came out slow and steady.

Some people thought he was bad, but others thought what? That he was good? "So, are you—" What was that word again? Oh yes—"a double agent?"

For once, he answered quickly. "I didn't say anything about being a double agent."

"But you implied it."

"No, you inferred it." His voice was louder now, as if I'd touched a nerve.

"Stop using lawyer talk," I begged. "Just tell me." Everything would make sense if he were a double agent.

He breathed out, long and hard. "I can't."

"Which means you're a double agent," I said, feeling certain I'd discovered the truth.

"All you need to know is that I can protect you. Other than that, I haven't told you anything." He looked at me as long as he could while driving. In his eyes, I saw fear. He was afraid I'd reveal his secret—that he was a good guy working for the bad guys.

Still, I needed to know more. "Are you working with the police? Or with the FBI?"

He didn't answer right away, confirming my hunch that I was on the right track. "I'm working with a federal agency, but I'm not one of their agents."

I stood up from the floor and sat on the passenger seat to get a better view of his face. "So that's why you don't want me to talk to the police—because you're in communication with this federal agency?"

Once again, he took his time answering. "Yes. They've been trying to catch your kidnappers for years. This armed robbery accusation is another one of their games."

I wasn't sure how accusing someone of a crime could qualify as a game, but then again, I hadn't understood much of what had happened over the past twenty-four hours. "What do you mean another one of their games?"

"They're trying to distract the police—make them believe you're the bad guy, so they don't believe your story about the kidnapping."

I wouldn't have believed him if it hadn't been for my experience talking to the police yesterday. I doubted I'd be any more convincing if I talked to them today. I was probably better off avoiding the police until Grant completed his undercover mission—if he really were on an undercover mission. "Is this like in *Rear Window*, where we need to gather evidence before the police will be able to help us?" As I said the words, they made sense to me. This could be the only way to put my kidnappers behind bars.

"That reminds me—the police are probably tracking your phone," Grant said. His voice was soft. "We should get rid of it."

I gripped the phone tighter in my hand. No way was I giving it up after all I'd done to find it again. Besides, it was just the thing a bad guy would tell me. "I'm going to have to think about that," I said.

"Okay." The way he said it, I could tell he'd expected me to respond the way I did.

I needed to know more about his undercover work in order to trust him. "So what do you know about Leslie Kaplan?"

He chuckled a little. "I guess if you want to go by Leslie's house, we can still do that. In fact, I think I need to pick something up there."

Ingrid and Ronald had kidnapped me because they thought I was Leslie, which meant she was probably a good guy. "I'd like to talk to her," I said, before realizing that was a stupid thing to say. She was probably in hiding if people wanted to kidnap her.

I needed to question Grant a little more—push him beyond the limits of an actor's knowledge. I wanted to make sure he was really the person I thought he was, and I was going to start with my area of expertise—old movies. "I have to confess you're the first guy I've ever met, except maybe my grandpa, who knows much about Grace Kelly. How many black-and-white movies have you seen?"

"That's hard to say. Maybe a hundred. Maybe more. My sister likes them too. You'll meet her if you come to Oklahoma. We used to have black-and-white-movie marathons every Saturday."

The fact that his sister loved old movies made it a little tempting to go to Oklahoma, but he could be making up a sister for that very purpose. I had to probe further. "What's your favorite black and white?"

"That'd be like asking a mother to choose a favorite child. There are too many good ones to choose a favorite."

"Okay, then. How about one you can recommend for me?"

"Oh, that's tough. You've probably seen the standards, like *Bringing Up Baby*, *It Happened One Night*, *I Remember Mama*."

"*I Remember Mama* is hardly a standard, but, yeah, I've seen it. I love everything with Irene Dunne."

"Ahh. Then you've seen *My Favorite Wife*?" The guy knew his stuff.

"Complete with knight-in-shining-armor scenes. I've also seen the remake with Doris Day." I couldn't remember what it was called, though.

"Oh, yeah. *Move Over Darling*. It had James Garner in it, didn't it?"

"That's it." I let myself lean back in my seat. He really wasn't faking about knowing his old movies. That was a relief. He couldn't be all that much of a bad guy if he liked to watch Irene Dunne.

"Here's one I'll bet you haven't seen," he said, his words picking up speed. *"Hobson's Choice.* It's an old British film. Kind of like *My Fair Lady,* only the woman sets out to reform the man. Have you seen it?"

"I don't think so, but I'll add it to my list."

I waited for him to say something about us watching it together, but that offer never came. He just kept his eyes on the road ahead.

I looked out the window as we entered a residential neighborhood. The houses were small, and the owners kept the lawns manicured. It was the type of trendy little neighborhood close to downtown where people tried hard to impress their neighbors—unlike in the country, where you could leave an old toilet out in the front yard for months without anyone noticing.

We stopped at one stop sign after another. It would have been easy for me to hop out at any time, but now I was curious to learn more about Leslie Kaplan.

For now, I was trusting Grant. He had said I was in danger, and the best way to safety was with him, but if he made one slip, I'd be off on my merry way to talk with the police like Wade had suggested.

"Do you live anywhere near here?" I asked.

"I have a condo on the other side of Houston."

That was progress. He'd given me some personal information, and I was about to ask him for his address when we pulled to a stop in front of a little house. I recognized it from the picture I'd seen on the internet—a white cottage with blue shutters and baskets of flowers hanging along the front porch.

Best of all, a woman—probably Leslie—had just pulled into the driveway and was getting out of her car.

CHAPTER 10

She was standing right there outside her house—the woman my kidnappers had mistaken me for. Only, she didn't look anything like me. Yes, she was blond, but that's where our similarities ended. She was much taller than I was, and her hair was long. She wasn't much of a vintage dresser either from the looks of the workout clothes she was wearing. Had she just come home from the gym?

As she walked to her front door, I jumped out of the truck and ran right up to her. "Ms. Kaplan?"

Loud barking came from the other side of the door, and she spoke soothingly toward it. "Hold on a minute Slurpee. I'm coming as fast as I can." Then she faced me. "I'm sorry, but I'm not Ms. Kaplan. I'm Bethany, her dog walker."

I stepped back. "Oh, pardon me." She looked much more like a Bethany than a Leslie.

She turned and put her key into the lock. "It's no problem. People mistake me for the homeowner all the time." Bethany turned the key in the lock and pushed the door open, allowing a black lab to bound outside. "You can ring the doorbell if you like."

Figuring it couldn't hurt anything, I rang the bell as Bethany entered the house. The dog's leash was the only thing hanging from the three hooks on the white wall. Bethany grabbed Slurpee's leash and attached it to his collar. Peeking in through the doorway, I saw a white couch and loveseat in the small living room, but there was no other clutter. The coffee table and end tables were bare. From what I could tell, Leslie Kaplan was a minimalist.

Bethany looked me up and down as she stepped back out the door, ready to walk the dog.

I stepped aside as she passed in between Grant and me. "What was it you needed to pick up?" I asked him.

His gaze darted from me to Bethany. "I'll get it later."

I was going to have to ask him more about Leslie, but first I needed to try a little harder with Bethany. This was probably my last chance to talk to her. I followed her down the sidewalk while Grant stood back and watched. "Could you tell me how I might get in touch with Leslie? Someone has mistaken me for her, and I'm in a lot of trouble because of it."

She pivoted toward me, and this time, I could tell something shifted inside her. "I once had the IRS audit me because someone else was using my social security number—the most stressful year of my life. I'm sorry I don't have Leslie's phone number, just an e-mail address. I've never actually met her. She's a good customer, though. Always pays me on time." She pulled out her phone to show me Leslie's e-mail address, which I hastily noted down on my phone as Bethany kept walking with the dog.

I ran to catch up with her and return her phone. "So you've never met Leslie in person?"

"Nope. I hate to say it, but she's exactly the type of person who shouldn't own a dog. She hires me to walk him twice a day seven days a week, but it's not the same for him as having an owner at home, you know?"

So Leslie needed a dog walker seven days a week. She was probably never home. "That's ... terrible."

"Yeah. Dogs are social creatures. They need to feel a part of a pack."

"How long have you worked for Leslie?"

"About six months."

I shivered a little, despite the heat. "That's a long time." Leslie had been in hiding for at least half a year.

"I'm sorry I can't tell you more," Bethany said as the dog tugged at the leash, trying to get her to keep walking down the sidewalk.

"No, no" I said, faking a polite smile despite my fear. "You've told me exactly what I need to know. Thank you."

CHAPTER 11

Knowing about Leslie Kaplan changed everything. If she was in hiding, I probably should be too. Which meant Grant's idea about me going to Oklahoma might not be a bad one. There was just one problem. I needed to know whether Grant was a good guy or a bad guy.

But how would I find that out? It wasn't like I could run a full background check on him. I couldn't take his fingerprints, and I didn't have access to any of his private information, unless …

As we walked back to the truck, I held out my hand. "This might be a weird request, but I'd like to see your wallet." There was no way I was getting back in that truck with him until I'd checked him out as thoroughly as possible.

He reached into his back pocket and pulled it out, but he didn't give it to me. "That's fine, but I have my own weird request—your phone. It'll be too easy to trace you with it."

"I can't give you my phone yet. I need it to look online and see if you have a criminal record."

He smiled and handed me his phone. "You can use mine. The password's RKT66."

I entered the password and put Grant Tilney in the search bar. Immediately, his professional website came up, advertising his work as a lawyer. So far, so good. "Okay," I said, "but don't do anything with my phone until I've checked you out."

He laughed at my accidental flirtation. "Check me out all you want. I have an account at backcheckusa.com if you'd like to use it."

I squinted at him through the sunlight. Was he trying to trick me with a fake website?"

"I used it when I was a lawyer. If you don't mind, we can use my password, and I can help you pull up my report. It wouldn't be a good idea for you to use your credit card."

We sat there in the shade of Leslie Kaplan's maple tree as Grant showed me how to search his criminal records, using his name and social security number. His record was squeaky clean, and I believed it. I opened his wallet and flipped to his driver's license, which was issued three years earlier and looked it. He had a beard in the picture. "How do I know this is your real name and social security number?"

"You don't." This was the part in old movies where the hero probably would have swept the heroine into his arms and kissed her. Ever after, she would trust him completely. Only, it didn't happen that way with Grant. He just shrugged. "You can call your brother to come pick you up if you'd like."

"I thought you said I was in danger."

"You are." The corners of his eyes pulled down, making him look like it hurt him to say it. "And you will be until we collect enough evidence to put your kidnappers behind bars, but it's your choice whether you want to come to Oklahoma with me or not."

So the truck driver job was just a cover for something bigger. His real job was collecting evidence. "What kind of evidence are we trying to collect against them?"

"I need to prove that they're trafficking illegal imports."

An illegal import that could be transported in a truck. That had to mean drugs. "Can't the police just bring in dogs to sniff out the drugs?"

"They could if the illegal imports were drugs. They're not. I have to collect the evidence myself if the feds are going to believe me."

Illegal imports that weren't drugs? What else could it be? Weapons?

I wanted to believe him. Unlike the police, he had trusted every word I said, and unlike everybody else, he understood how dangerous my mysterious kidnappers had been. How could I not trust him back? I handed him my phone. "What are you going to do with this?"

"See how the dog walker left her windows cracked," he said, pointing to her car. He stood and slipped the phone through the crack. "She'll be driving this to the other side of Houston in a few minutes. It'll throw everybody off our track, which is exactly what you need. I promise I'll get you a new one when this is all over."

85

CHAPTER 12

I peered through the window at my phone, now laying on the back seat of the dog walker's car and kicked my foot against the tire. I'd loved that phone—bought with my very first paycheck from my job as a receptionist at the city hall. Grant had better be right about me needing to lose it.

I shuffled through the rest of the cards from his wallet—two credit cards, insurance cards, a couple of store cards, and one that showed he was an Eagle Scout. That was what did it—that Eagle Scout card. It was just too perfect. I had five brothers, and even more guy friends, yet I had never in my life known a guy as perfect as Grant. Not even Ryan Shumway, the guy I dated during my freshman year of college, who owned a lawncare business and ran marathons. From a distance, he seemed like a great boyfriend, but in reality, he smelled like gasoline, judged me for eating cheeseburgers, and lied to his mother.

Nope, I just couldn't believe the whole lawyer, truck driver, and Eagle scout combination, especially now that he'd taken my phone from me. "I'm not going with you to Oklahoma," I told him. "And I want my phone back." This was the right decision. It was the logical thing to do. Everybody knew it was always best to go to the police. The truth would prevail and all that. Besides, my parents would have completely freaked out if I'd spent the night at his house in Oklahoma.

He raked a hand through his hair as he stood next to me, leaning against the dog walker's car. "Now you tell me. Five seconds after I dropped it."

"More like thirty seconds." I gave him back his wallet and phone. "I'll just wait around and get my phone when the dog walker gets back."

His eyebrows pulled down. "Are you sure?"

My heart so wanted me to say I wasn't sure, that I was terrified of being kidnapped again or of having another police officer think I was crazy. My heart would have rather spent the next few hours flirting with Grant in his truck, but my head just couldn't let me go on in this fantasy. "I'm positive." I turned my gaze down the street, so I wouldn't see the disappointment in his eyes. "I want you to leave me here."

"I'm not going to leave you here," I heard him say. "I've got to wait around to get Slurpee."

My gaze snapped back to meet his. Yes, the dog seemed lonely, but that didn't justify kidnapping him. "What do you mean get Slurpee?"

He stared up at the sky for a few seconds and then sighed as his gaze returned to meet mine. "I might as well tell you. Leslie's not a real person. She's a decoy. I rented this house in her name, got her a phone, an e-mail address, and a dog to throw the bad guys off my scent. But all it's done is gotten you in trouble and made Slurpee the loneliest dog ever. I'm going to take him home to my dad's house in Oklahoma when he gets back from his walk."

I giggled. It was just like something out of a movie. "Seriously?" If I knew for sure that he'd been pretending to be Leslie Kaplan for the last six months, that would be all the proof I needed to trust him completely. "Can you prove that you created Leslie Kaplan?" I asked.

He pulled another phone from his pocket, one he hadn't shown me before, and entered the password. "This is Leslie's."

Putting his phone into my pocket, I searched the various applications on Leslie's phone, finding her e-mails, her texts, and her voicemail messages. I even found her bank account, which included recurring payments to Bethany, the dog walker. "How did you manage to open a bank account without any form of ID?"

"My government contacts helped me out."

I grinned at him. That was it. I had to believe him.

The funny thing was, though, that he didn't grin back. The expression on his face reminded me of the time my brother broke his leg in the football game but didn't want to cry in front of his teammates.

I was in bigger trouble than I wanted to believe. We both were.

I handed Grant back Leslie's phone, and, as I did, the phone in my pocket buzzed.

In my distraction, I answered it. "Hello ... Mr. Tilney's phone." I'd spent three years as a receptionist, and it showed.

"Oh," a female voice on the other end answered. She was probably his girlfriend. He'd never told me about her, of course. He was a spy, after all. There had to be so much about him that he hadn't told me. "You must be Eva."

So he'd told his girlfriend about me? That didn't make sense. "Yes, I'm Eva. Who's this?"

"It's Sophia. Grant's sister."

Grant's sister, the one who liked movies. I'd forgotten about her. "Oh, it's nice to meet you. I was just calling because Grant texted that he was bringing you home for a visit, but, typical of him, he didn't give us any details." It sounded like something I would say about one of my brothers.

"So he isn't as perfect as he seems."

High-pitched laughter sounded from the other end of the phone. "Are you kidding me? The other day he was complaining that his chicken noodle soup was too salty. I had to teach him that you don't eat condensed soup straight. You add a can of water. And don't get me started on his lack of communication. He'll talk my ear off about politics and the Constitution, but he doesn't bother to let us know when he plans to arrive at our house. Is it today, tomorrow, next week, or next month?"

"I totally understand. I have a brother like that too." I smiled at Grant, but his eyes were scanning the street, looking for danger. "Your sister wants to know when you're planning to get to Oklahoma."

He grabbed hold of my arm and tilted his head toward the backyard. "I think it's safer back there."

After we slipped through the fence and hid behind a bush, he took the phone from me. "We should get there around midnight," he told Sophia. "Don't stress about it." He paused, listening and then responded. "It's not that exactly. She's gotten mixed up in that project I've been working on." He paused again, and I strained to hear what Sophia said in response, but it was too muffled. "No," he said, "the secret project." He heaved a sigh. "I know I shouldn't have gotten her involved. It just happened, okay?"

Hearing him talk about me that way, I couldn't help getting tears in my eyes. It was so frustrating that everyone—even Grant's sister—understood more about my situation than I did. And yet, I was the one who'd gotten kidnapped, I was the one in trouble with the police, and I was the one who couldn't go back home.

He glanced sideways at me as I tried to blink back the tears. "Look," he told Sophia, "I've gotta go. See you tonight." He dropped the phone and took my hand in his. "It's going to be okay. We got them off our track when I let them search the truck cab. You did a great job hiding."

I sniffled. "Thanks." At least I'd done that one thing right.

He rubbed his thumb along the back of my hand. "What exactly did she tell you?"

I laughed through my sniffles, remembering my conversation with Sophia. "She told me how you ate condensed soup without adding water."

His face went beet red. "She promised she wouldn't tell anyone about that."

I squeezed his hand. "Trust me. It was just what I needed to hear."

He leaned back against a wooden fence that was behind us and shook his head. "I think you two are going to have fun together."

I sniffled again. That was right. I still needed to decide whether to go to Oklahoma with him. "I wish I knew more about everything that's going on," I said, hoping he'd tell me all the details.

"I know it's frustrating," he said, giving me a weak smile, "but believe me, it's better if you don't know. The more you know, the more you'll want to get involved, and I don't want you any more involved than you already are."

That made sense. It also showed that Grant understood me. Once I became passionate about something, I couldn't resist doing whatever I could to help the cause—often forgetting caution. The safe thing would be for me to hunker down in Oklahoma until Grant finished his secret mission. "Will you at least explain everything to me when it's over?" I asked. I couldn't stand the idea of never knowing.

He blinked, as if he hadn't expected me to say that. "Yes. Definitely."

"How long will I have to stay in Oklahoma?" I could only imagine how much my parents were already freaking out. I didn't want to prolong their agony more than was necessary.

"No longer than a week. I'll try to make it sooner."

We waited behind the bush until Bethany came back, put the dog inside, and left in her car (which still had my phone inside.) Then Grant took a key from his pocket, opened the backdoor with it, and walked back outside, holding a bag of dog food in one hand and the end of Slurpee's leash in the other. Slurpee strained at the leash, his tongue hanging out. He was ready for an adventure.

Trying to look natural, we walked Slurpee back to the truck, and I sat with the poor dog in the passenger seat as we drove out of the neighborhood, his body trembling as he stared out the window. "I can't tell if he's nervous or excited," I said. "When was the last time he got to go for a ride?"

Grant's shoulders slumped as he started the engine. "When I brought him here from the shelter," he said. "It's been about nine months. Way too long."

I could tell he thought I was judging him. "Don't feel too bad," I said. "He's had two walks a day for all that time."

Grant's shoulders lifted a little as he glanced across at the dog. "He'll be happier with Sophia in Oklahoma."

"I'm looking forward to meeting Sophia in person. I'm also excited to meet your dad."

The light changed and he pulled the truck forward. "I should warn you. Dad's not a people person."

"I'll bet he's a lot like my dad—kind of the scholarly, quiet type?" I asked, hoping he'd elaborate.

"No. He's the cranky-old-man type."

Great. As if I hadn't had enough cranky people around me for one day! I petted Slurpee's soft fur as he rested his paws on the windowsill. At least I'd have the dog to help me relax. "Speaking of dads," I said, "is there any way I can let my parents know I'm okay?" I still had Grant's phone in my pocket. It'd be easy enough to send them an e-mail.

Grant tensed his jaw as he drove through the quiet neighborhood. "Let's take a minute and think about whether that's a good idea."

That must have meant it was a bad idea. "Where are we going anyway? All I know is that it's in Oklahoma."

The tension left his face as he reached for the radio dial and turned on some soft music. "After I pick up my trailer load, we're heading to a little town named Northanger. It's way out in the country."

"Northanger. Cool name. It sounds like a place where you'd find dragons and castles."

"Yeah. It sounds that way, doesn't it? But you're more likely to catch chiggers than dragons. And my father's house is large, but it's not a castle. My mother used to call it an estate."

"An estate?" I'd never been to an estate, but it was definitely the kind of place I'd always wanted to visit—a large, spacious mansion with a swirling staircase in the entryway and numerous rooms to wander through, all with names from the game of Clue: the conservatory, the library, the dining room. I imagined Grant's father sitting by a fireplace in the sitting room. Hanging above the fireplace, would be a giant portrait of the estate's original owner. Estates were the kinds of places that were ripe with mysteries.

"It used to look like an estate too, but since my parents divorced it's become a bit of a mess. You'll see when we get there."

"Oh," I said, reaching to touch his arm. "I'm sorry your parents are divorced." His mom, at least, sounded fun—decorating the house like an estate—compared to the father, who wasn't a people person, but it was clear I wouldn't be meeting her.

He pushed his sunglasses up higher on his nose. "I used to be sorry about the divorce too, but the older I get, the more I see that it was inevitable."

91

Inevitable? Was his father abusive? Or the mother perhaps too extravagant?

He heaved a sigh. "I just wish I could convince my sister that it was inevitable."

I had to hide in the back of the cab while Grant picked up his trailer near the same warehouse where I'd met Ingrid and Ronald, but when we were back on the road, I sat in the front again.

"I've got a few audiobooks downloaded on my phone," Grant said. "Maybe we could listen to one of them. They're on a library app. I forget what it's called."

Since his phone was still in my pocket, I got it out and found what he was talking about. "Hey, I use this same app. It's funny. I thought you'd be the type to buy your audiobooks."

"I sometimes go shopping for paperbacks, but I usually end up buying overpriced cheesecake and chocolate truffles instead of books."

I laughed. "I usually end up with an inspiring quote magnet for my fridge."

He raised his eyebrows and deadpanned. "Not a sterling silver bookmark or a bust of Mr. Darcy?"

"No, but I was once tempted by a gold-plated pen." The bookshelf on his phone opened, and I found three books ready to listen to—an Agatha Christy mystery novel, *The BFG* by Roald Dahl, and a nonfiction book about the battle of Bunker Hill. "Normally, I'd be all for listening to this Agatha Christy, but today, I'd prefer Roald Dahl's Big Friendly Giant. Are you up for *The BFG*?"

"I'm always up for *The BFG*," Grant said. "He's sort of my soulmate, rescuing the world one dream at a time."

It took me a while to process what he'd said. "Is that what you're doing, rescuing the world?" I didn't mention my theory again that he was a double agent, but that's what I was thinking.

"I don't know if I'm doing it, but that's my goal."

"Okay," I said, "here we go then." I tapped *The BFG*.

We laughed our way through all four and a half hours of the audiobook, pausing only once at a truck stop to fuel up, buy some snacks, and use the restrooms.

When it was over, the sun was beginning to set, and I was ready for a nap, but Grant had something else in mind. "How about we play the alphabet game?" By the way he said it, I knew he wasn't serious. He probably hated the game.

Since I grew up as the middle child in a family of ten, I had to agree that the alphabet game was one of the worst. "How about twenty questions instead?"

"Okay," he said, "I'll start. I'm thinking of a celebrity."

"Is he male?" I asked, already bored with this idea.

"Yes."

I didn't feel like talking about celebrities, not when there was so much more I needed to know about Grant. "Are you from Texas?"

"I don't know. How is that relevant, anyway?"

"I'm asking about you, not the celebrity. It's a yes or no question. Are you from Texas?"

"I guess I'll allow it," he said, sounding like a judge. "No."

"Are you from Oklahoma?"

"Yes."

"Hmm. Why don't you have an accent then? You don't even say y'all."

"Yes or no questions, Eva," he repeated, his voice quiet, yet stern.

By this time, I was convinced that he really was a lawyer. "Okay, sorry. Did you ever live anywhere other than Oklahoma?"

"Yes."

"Was it another state or another country?"

"Yes to both questions."

I spent the next few minutes naming states and countries until I figured out he'd lived in Michigan and Mexico, quite the combination of climates. "Was this while you still lived with your parents?"

"Yes."

That meant his parents probably worked for the CIA. "Did one of your parents work for the government?"

"No," he replied, not that he could tell me if they did work for the government. They probably pretended to work in a different profession.

"So they were in business down in Mexico?"

"Yes."

"Trucking?" I asked. That waitress had told me his family owned a trucking company, but she could have been mistaken.

"No," he replied.

I'd have to figure out later how he got into trucking. For now, I needed to know more about Mexico. "Were you very young when you lived in Mexico?"

"I went to third through sixth grade there." He was merging into another lane because of construction and must have forgotten about the yes-or-no-questions rule. Or maybe he was just as tired of the format as I was.

I wasn't going to remind him to stick to the rules. "So you speak Spanish?"

"I went to an English-speaking school, but I learned enough Spanish to get by in the city."

"Mexico City?"

"Yes."

I wondered if that was before his parents' divorce but decided it would be rude to ask directly. I was already pushing my limits. "Do your parents speak Spanish too?"

"My mom does. Dad never bothered to learn."

So it sounded like he was past elementary school when his parents split up.

"How about you?" he asked. "Have you lived anywhere other than Texas?"

"No. I've always lived in the same town, same house, even the same bedroom. Boring, huh?"

"Lucky, I'd say. I wouldn't mind living in the country for the rest of my life. When I was a kid, my dream was to live somewhere with my own fishing pond. You don't happen to have one of those, do you?"

"We have a pond, but there aren't any fish in it." Now we were getting somewhere. I wondered if his dream included a wife and children. "I always dreamed of helping orphans in India."

He nodded. "I like that idea. Would you ever want to adopt a child from another country?"

That was exactly my dream, but I didn't want to sound too eager. Then again, he might as well know the truth. "Actually, I've spent a lot of time learning about international adoption. There are so many children who need families."

"True," he said, "most people would prefer not to think about it."

"Well, I'm not like most people, and I don't think you are either."

He shook his head, chuckling. "No, I'm like most people. That's why I need people like you to remind me of the bigger causes in the world. Sophia's like you that way. Her college major is something called 'conflict resolution.' She's hoping to end some of the conflict in the Middle East."

I had to hand it to Sophia. That was a bigger goal than I'd ever had. Still, it didn't seem that different from the type of thing Grant was doing. "I'm sure she wasn't at all inspired by her secret agent brother."

"I'm really proud of her," Grant said, ignoring my compliment. "She does anything she sets her mind to. She can make furniture, jewelry, clothes—and she can grow anything. You'll see when we get there. She's always out working in her gardens."

It was night by the time we came to the forested area around Northanger. Large trees hovered over the road, making the night seem even darker. The few houses we passed along the way didn't strike me as places of wealth. They seemed more like backwoods shacks.

After turning down a long, winding asphalt drive, we pulled to a stop in a large, circular driveway—just big enough for Grant to turn around his big rig. As soon as I opened my door, the dog bounded out, and I scrambled to grab the end of the leash. He sniffed at a bush while I admired the front garden, which sparkled with hundreds of solar-powered lights. I could tell this was Sophia's English-style garden. In the center stood a large fountain surrounded by a brick walkway. Circling out from around the fountain were rings of flowers, all enclosed within a low, boxwood hedge.

Behind the garden, loomed a tall house. It was only after we walked through the garden that I noticed its stone walls and paneled windows. Flanking each side of the house were what must have been newer additions, so many that the place seemed more like a military installation than an estate. It also seemed there was plenty of work to do. My parents would have had all us kids out scrubbing stains from the stone walls and replacing the cracked window glass. Just when I was contemplating how long it would take to whip the place into shape, a dark-haired woman emerged from the darkness. "You two got here faster than I thought." I recognized her voice immediately. It was Sophia.

"What are you doing out so late?" Grant called.

She held a flashlight in one hand and a backpack in the other. Her hair grew in frizzy waves. "Wishing on shooting stars. I've seen three so far tonight."

He placed an arm around my shoulder. "I know you two have already met on the phone, but this is Eva."

She flashed a broad smile and extended her hand to me. "Nice to meet you, Eva."

"Nice to meet you too," I said, meaning every word.

Sophia's smile reassured me. "We'll have a fun time together. There are tons of things we can do around the house and grounds." In the dim glow of the porch light, she studied the clothes I was wearing—Grant's clothes. "Remind me later, and I'll wash a load of clothes for you before I go to bed. I'll also get you some pajamas you can borrow."

Grant motioned toward the dog. "And this is Slurpee."

"You got a dog?" Sophia asked as she bent to let Slurpee sniff her hand and then petted him. "I thought you couldn't have pets when you were driving your truck."

Grant hesitated. "I thought Slurpee could stay with you."

Sophia laughed. "Does Dad know about your plan?"

"I'll talk to him." Grant pushed open the door, and we stepped inside a large room, which was decorated in a mix of styles. The sofa hailed from the nineties while the jungle paintings on the wall had to be from South America. A shaker-style rocker sat next to a colonial-style armoire. Under the far window, three empty birdcages sat on a table.

Sophia gripped her hands in front of her. "You guys must be starving after that long drive." She rose onto her tiptoes and pivoted toward an exit at the far side of the room. "Lucky for you I've got all the ingredients to make cherry blintzes."

Grant leaned toward me. "Crepes with a creamy filling," he whispered.

"Oh, I love crepes," I said, trying to regain my enthusiasm about this visit.

"Sophia's the best crepe-maker I know. She can show you how to make them if you want."

"That'd be fantastic." My previous attempts at making crepes had ended with thick blobs of batter. But all I really wanted to know was what she knew about Grant's secret project.

I followed Grant and Sophia through a hallway, past a dining room, and into what looked like a newer addition of the house. The kitchen was large enough for an estate with its two big gas stoves and twelve-foot-long counter, not to mention all the cabinets. While Grant filled a bowl of water for Slurpee, Sophia pulled a frying pan from one of the cabinets. She opened a refrigerator that looked large enough to serve a restaurant and pulled out a dish of butter, some eggs, and a gallon of milk.

As she mixed the eggs and milk, Grant set the bowl of water down for the dog and then opened the refrigerator to inspect its contents. "No meat, no cheese, no fruits, no vegetables. I guess I'll be shopping."

A deep voice bellowed from the far side of the room. "You'll do no such thing. I'll go shopping tomorrow morning."

It was as if an icy wind had blasted through the warm atmosphere of the room. Sophia dropped her whisk, and Grant let the refrigerator door close. All was quiet except for Slurpee lapping his water. I turned to see the man I presumed to be Grant's

97

father, a tall thin man with thinning grey hair. He was dressed formally for an evening at home with his dress shirt buttoned one button from the top.

Grant straightened his back. "Yes, sir." Then he stepped toward me. "Dad, I'd like to introduce you to Eva Morland. Eva, this is my father, Mr. Tilney."

Mr. Tilney looked me up and down. "Pleased to meet you, Miss Morland," he droned without a smile.

"I also brought a dog home," Grant said.

Mr. Tilney frowned. "I noticed." He turned to me again. "What is it you do, Miss Morland?"

I pasted on a smile and injected cheer into my voice. "I'm a college student, studying forensic science. I work part-time as a receptionist at my local town hall, and I'm also a vlogger—I make video blogs."

"Video blogs?" he asked, making it sound like that was a bad thing.

"Yes, sir," I replied, "My biggest fans are teenage girls, so I don't think you'd be interested in them—unless you want to channel the younger, more feminine version of yourself." His face remained stoic, so I huffed out a laugh to show I was kidding.

He frowned. "Sophia, please show Eva where she can sleep—above the garage." He stopped and stared at the dog, his lips twisting. "While you're at it, take the dog to the garage. I won't have it wandering through the house at night." Then he turned and walked back out the kitchen door. Grant was right. He was cranky.

CHAPTER 13

Sophia knocked on my door early the next morning, and by early, I mean before the sun came up. "I've got your clean clothes, and I was wondering if you want to eat breakfast with us before Grant leaves."

I sat bolt upright in bed. Grant was leaving. "Yes," I called, prying myself out of bed.

When I cracked open the door, Slurpee nudged his way inside, sniffing at my legs.

"Okay," Sophia said, handing me a stack of folded clothes. "I'll wait for you at the bottom of the stairs."

The room where Mr. Tilney had me sleep was over the detached garage. It was spacious, and included not only a bed, but also its own sofa, TV, video game console, and pool table, as well as a full bathroom, where I'd showered the night before. I guessed that Grant's father wanted to keep me as far as possible from his son, but I couldn't be sure. Perhaps, he felt this was the nicest guest room.

And it was a nice room—very comfortable ... except for one thing. It had one of those deer heads mounted on the wall. I could feel its beady eyes watching me as I slipped into my newly cleaned dress—the same one I'd been wearing when I did the videos with Clayton. Since the kidnappers had taken my purse, I didn't have any make-up. All I could do was comb my hair, wash my face, and brush my teeth with the toothbrush Sophia had given me the night before. It took all of five minutes before Slurpee and I were running down the stairs to meet Sophia, who led us back inside the main house.

The dining room was dimly lit with wood paneling and antique, mahogany furniture. Four plates of omelets lay on the table. Mr. Tilney sat at the head.

"Good morning," I said.

"Good morning," he replied, not sounding at all like he felt it to be true.

Grant still hadn't arrived. Sophia pointed out a chair for me. When I sat on the upholstered seat, it creaked, and the back leaned too much to be comfortable, so I sat as straight as I could, which was probably good manners anyway. Slurpee sat on the floor beside my chair, just like my dog Ozzy did at home. He probably expected some table scraps. I would have to ask Grant later where he put the dog food.

Sophia sat on my left farther down the table. "It is a nice morning, isn't it?" she said. "Not quite as humid as yesterday. The sky was so clear last night, I felt sure today would be gorgeous."

I agreed with her while at the same time, trying to remember all the rules of etiquette my parents had taught me.

Grant came in, his hair wet and wavy from the shower. "Morning, Dad." He smiled to Sophia and me. "Morning, Eva, Sophia. You both look beautiful, but I hope you didn't wake up early for my sake." Slurpee wandered over to greet Grant, abandoning me.

"We wanted to see you off," Sophia said.

"Where are you heading on this next trip," Mr. Tilney asked, lifting his fork. "Or can you tell us?"

Before I had much time to wonder why Grant would have to keep his trucking route secret, Grant answered. "I'm heading up to the Dakotas this time.

The Dakotas! That would take a while.

"Well," Mr. Tilney said, "we might as well start eating. Grant needs to get on the road. This little detour has already cost him too much time."

I took a bite of omelet. Was Mr. Tilney blaming me for Grant's detour? The way he narrowed his eyes at me told me he did.

"I've always wanted to go up there," Sophia said, sounding as cheerful as possible, given the somber mood cast over the room by her father. "Someday you'll have to take me, Grant."

"I don't think that's a good idea," Mr. Tilney muttered.

Instead of defending her idea, Sophia simply shrugged. "No. I guess not." It made me wonder if she had health problems Grant hadn't told me about.

Silence fell on the room as I tried to estimate how long it would take Grant to drive his big rig to the Dakotas and back. It seemed like I would probably be here for most of the week. The more I thought about it, the darker the room seemed to grow. Was I going to be able to talk to him alone before he left?

"I watched a couple of your little videos, Ms. Morland," Mr. Tilney said.

I struggled to swallow another bite of omelet. These were the kinds of words that chilled me to the bone, even more so because I liked his son so much. "Really? Which ones did you see?" I didn't dare ask if he liked them.

"The ones you most recently posted with that young man."

Young man? I never posted videos with a young man.

"You were talking about your kidnapping," he prodded.

Heat rushed to my face. "Oh, you mean the live videos I did with Clayton." I took a sip of orange juice. "Clayton is my brother's friend." By that, I hoped to imply that I had no romantic connection with Clayton. I didn't want him to think I was some boy-crazy college girl who chased after a new man every day.

Grant broke in. "These omelets are really great, Dad."

"They are wonderful," I agreed, though I'd hardly tasted them. My mind had been so occupied.

"We raise our own chickens," Sophia added, turning to me. "Can you taste the difference?"

"Definitely," I said, forcing enthusiasm into my voice.

"Dad runs a tight ship," Grant explained, pointing to a dish of salsa. "He also bottled the salsa."

Mr. Tilney lifted his chin. "I like to be self-sufficient."

The room fell silent for a few minutes as we ate, but it was so silent I couldn't stand it. I had to think of something to say. As I finished off my omelet, I thought of how Grant's father was self-sufficient, he raised chickens, and bottled salsa. Come on, Eva, say something. I remembered the deer head in my room. "Do you hunt your own meat, Mr. Tilney?"

He shook his head. "No. My hunting days are over."

"Thank you for breakfast, Dad," Grant said, wiping his lips with his napkin and then placing it beside his plate on the table. He looked at his watch. "I guess I'd better get going." He turned to me. "Would you like to see me off, Eva?"

I nodded. "Yes."

Everyone at the table stood as Grant and I got up to go. With the dog in tow, we walked together out to his truck, which was still parked in the driveway. "I'm going to miss you, Eva Morland," he said, letting go of Slurpee's leash and ordering him to stay.

"Not as much as I'll miss you." Tears didn't come to my eyes, but my voice definitely betrayed me. I sounded as emotional as a seventh-grade girl.

He dropped his duffle bag beside the truck and hooked his thumbs through his belt loops. "You'll have fun with Sophia at least."

I sighed. "Yes, I like Sophia. I'm just a little worried about your father. I don't think he likes me at all."

"He comes across as gruff, but he's really not that bad. He'll keep you safe here. That's what matters. Once I'm back on the road, I'll have someone pass the word along to your parents that you're okay."

I threw my arms around him, pressing my face into the crook under his chin. "I still wish you wouldn't go."

He hugged me tight, and I felt his lips press against the top of my hair. How could I ever feel safer than this? "I don't know why I trust you so much," I whispered. "There's just something inside me. It's like a magnet, telling me to stay as close to you as possible."

"I've got the same magnet inside of me," he said.

I giggled, pulling back. It was the first time he didn't sound at all like a lawyer. That had to mean I was cracking through his outer layers. I peered up into his eyes. "Technically, you would have the opposite magnet inside you … or maybe the same one but upside down."

He took hold of my hands. "I don't feel like we're all that different."

"I hope the pull is enough to make you come back as soon as possible."

"I will. You don't have to worry about that." He gave both my hands a squeeze. Then he let go, hopped into the truck, and while I stood watching, he drove off.

I sniffled a bit and blinked away the tears. Then I squared my shoulders, took a deep breath, and looked around. The estate was different by the light of the morning. The garden burst forth in a rainbow of color. Birds sang. A slight breeze blew, bringing with it the sweet fragrance of rose bushes. Slurpee sniffed at a nearby lavender plant. Sure, the paint on the house was chipped and crumbling, and two of the windows were covered with plywood, but I really had no reason to feel trepidation about staying here.

Sophia must have been watching from inside because after Grant's truck disappeared, she walked out the front door. "I take a walk every morning after breakfast. Would you like to join me today?"

"I'd love to."

Grabbing onto Slurpee's leash, I followed her around the corner of the house, where she pointed out a row of trees. "These are Dad's peach trees." She pointed out the blossoms that grew along their branches. "Peach pie is his favorite."

Around toward the back, we came upon a large red chicken coop enclosed in a chicken wire pen. The construction looked new and included a door for people to go in and out. "Dad's already been out to feed them and gather their eggs."

"What does your father do?"

She looked at me, her face questioning.

"I mean, what does he do for a living?"

"Oh." She stared down at the ground. "He runs his own business. It's quite complicated. He's sort of a consultant. He used to travel a lot for his work. He even has his own plane, but now that Grant's so busy, he doesn't fly much."

That was vague. "Does Grant travel in his place?"

"No, it's just that Dad won't go anywhere unless Grant can come stay with me."

Sophia was twenty-one, old enough to stay at home by herself. Her father sounded much more protective than my parents had ever been. "I guess that's what happens when you're the only daughter," I said, hoping she'd explain more about her unusual father.

She rolled her eyes. "Yeah. I've never spent a night away from him—no college dorm visits, no slumber parties, no trips with friends."

"Why not?"

She shook her head. "He says it's too dangerous."

The sun shone down on the creek as I skipped another rock. What could be so dangerous about a slumber party? Then I remembered—Sophia knew about Grant's secret project. Had my kidnappers threatened her?

We crossed a field to a wooded area. There, just a few feet beyond the trees, Sophia led me to a wide creek that looked like it had at least a foot of water in it. "This is my favorite place," she said, perching on a large rock and skipping a stone across the water. "Grant and I used to spend hours and hours out here. We got so muddy. Mom hated it."

I found a rock close by to sit on. "So your mom lived here in Northanger with you?"

Sophia threw another stone, but this one landed with a plunk. "Yes, for a few years. I was pretty young when she left. Grant remembers her better than I do."

"You mean you don't keep in touch?" I asked, wondering why Grant had never mentioned this strange consequence of his parents' divorce.

She shook her head before skipping another stone over the water. "I haven't seen her or talked to her since I was seven." She spoke through her teeth, her words grating together. "One night, she tucked me into bed and told me to always be a good girl. Grant and I heard her and Dad yelling at each other later on. That happened a lot, but always in the morning, things were back to normal. Not this time, though. In the morning, Mom had left. And she's never come back."

"You mean you don't know anything about your mom anymore?" I asked, thinking she had to be exaggerating.

104

Sophia stared down at the creek bank. "For all I know, she could be dead."

Goosebumps crept up my arms. Sophia's mother left one morning, and they'd never heard from her since then? It must have been some fight.

A cold breeze blew across the creek and I folded my arms, attempting to warm myself. What if the fight between Mr. and Mrs. Tilney had gotten physical, and Mrs. Tilney had left because she was being abused? That couldn't be, though. She wouldn't have left her children behind if she had been trying to escape from abuse.

CHAPTER 14

I had just gotten up my courage to ask Sophia more about the last time she saw her mother, but she spoke first. "Grant tells me you like old movies." She stood up from the rock and turned toward the house.

I skipped one more stone across the creek. "Yep. He told me you like them too."

She gestured for me to follow her. We walked back across the field and entered the house from the back, where Sophia showed me the living room. It was probably the most normal-looking room I'd seen so far in the house—tan carpet, brown sofa, brown chairs, a wide-screen TV, and three bookshelves that contained both DVDs and books. I probably could have found a similar room in about 25 percent of the homes in America.

"What are you in the mood for today?" she asked, waving her hands at the bookshelves. "We've got a huge selection, and it doesn't matter to me which one you pick. I have to do my homework while I'm watching."

That was right—homework. If I weren't on spring break, I'd be doing homework too. "You don't have to watch for my benefit. I mean, if you need to do homework, you can go somewhere quieter." The last thing I wanted was to be a bother. I remembered that old saying by Ben Franklin about how guests start to smell like fish if they stay longer than three days—or something like that.

She plopped into an armchair and opened her laptop. "I always do homework while I'm watching TV. The house is so quiet, I need noise to help me sit still, so you being here will be good for my grades."

It was the exact opposite of the way it was for me—I needed quiet, which was always hard to find in my house—but she seemed to be telling the truth, so I walked over to peruse the DVD titles on the bookshelf. They had almost all of my favorites, as well as a lot that most people our age had probably never even heard of. I found the one Grant had recommended to me, *Hobson's Choice*, and popped it into the DVD player.

As the movie began, my gaze wandered to the walls around us. There were pictures of Grant and Sophia when they were younger, including an adorable photo of Grant as a toddler. He was standing on a city street that must have been in Mexico and holding Mexican street corn. I scanned the background for any sign of his mother. Then I looked at the other pictures. Mr. Tilney was in some of the photos, but Grant and Sophia's mother wasn't in any of them. I would have liked to have known what she looked like.

I watched the movie without talking because as much as I believed Sophia needed the noise, I also guessed that any chatter from me probably wouldn't help her get her projects done.

It was just the type of movie my mom and dad would have loved, and once again, I felt a pang of homesickness. When would I get to see my family again, and what must they think about all the criminal charges against me? It was all so real to me—meeting Grant in the diner, attempting to return his phone, getting kidnapped, escaping, talking to the police, hitting Ingrid over the head, and asking Grant to help me—it all made sense from my point of view, but I doubted it would to my parents. They probably thought I'd gone crazy. I hoped Grant had found some way to let them know I was safe, so they wouldn't worry so much.

The movie had a girl-power theme, and I liked Grant even more for recommending a movie that showed a woman who could not only get out from under her father's oppressive rule, but could also build her own business. The father was so grouchy, I thought again of Sophia's strange relationship with her father.

It was odd that Sophia had never spent the night away from home. Surely, she'd have had to attend an orientation somewhere for her college program. "Where do you go to school again?" I asked.

She looked up from her laptop and smiled, seeming happy to be interrupted. "Eastern Allegheny University."

I wasn't sure where Allegheny was. "That's pretty far away, right?" I asked.

She shrugged. "It's in Pennsylvania. They're the only online school that has a degree in conflict resolution. That's why I picked them."

I took my time responding, trying my best not to make it sound like I disapproved of her choices. "That must save a lot of money … since you don't have to travel. Not that I think you're poor or anything." The longer I spoke, the worse this was getting. "I just—"

"—You feel sorry for me, never leaving this house." She was staring back down at the screen of her laptop. "It's okay. I have a lot of hobbies."

As unfair as my life seemed right then, at least I'd had plenty of freedom to get out and meet people before Mrs. Garland went and kidnapped me. Sophia had been dealing with this sort of thing for her entire life. In a week or so when it was all over for me, Sophia would probably still be sitting at home, taking online classes.

I turned my attention back to the movie, where the characters were opening their own little shoe shop and selling fashionable footwear. Grant was right. I loved the movie. For an hour and a half, I almost forgot I was so far from home. Seeing all the costumes made me want to go shopping, though—like serious vintage clothes shopping—and shopping far from home was the best. I'd heard of people finding serious stuff in Oklahoma thrift shops—the types of things that had been hanging around in Grandma's closet for half a century, which meant I was likely to find the types of things Grace Kelly would have worn. Sophia and I needed to go on an excursion.

Once the movie ended, I couldn't help asking, "Are there any thrift stores around here?"

Sophia peeked at me over the top of her laptop. "Oh, no you don't. Grant told me it's not safe for you to leave the house. Besides, I have to stay here in the house or on the grounds. It's the rules."

"You mean, you can never go shopping?" Mr. Tilney was grumpy, but he couldn't be that strict.

"Only when my dad or Grant come along." She spoke as if it were no big deal. As if she'd been living this way for her entire life, like Rapunzel in a tower.

Maybe she didn't mind keeping the rules, but I was a free woman. How dangerous could it be to visit a thrift store? "I can't just keep wearing this same dress every day. And don't tell me I can borrow your clothes. Your pajamas were way too small."

"Hmm." She looked at my dress. "We have some clothes out in the garage. Dad never throws anything out."

Dad never throws anything out. That was normally just the sort of thing I loved to hear. On this occasion, however, I couldn't help feeling a little apprehensive. Exactly whose clothes had he saved? His wife's? And how would he feel about me wearing them? I could imagine that seeing someone else in his ex-wife's clothes could cause a certain amount of instability.

"Are you sure your dad will approve?"

But Sophia had already jumped up off the sofa and was heading out of the room. "Come on. We've got some pretty cool stuff. Even if you don't find something you like, it's at least entertaining."

She took me back to the garage, but this time instead of climbing the stairs to my room, we entered the side door into the garage. A very old hatchback sat parked next to an almost-as-old luxury sedan. Around them, stuffed animals lined the walls, but not the cuddly kind—the dead animal kind, stuffed by a taxidermist. At least ten exotic birds stared at me from over the top of two chest freezers, a jaguar loomed in the corner, and a monkey stood frozen in time on the top of a shelf. I stuck close to Sophia's side and pretended it was the most normal thing in the world to encounter dead animals in a garage.

Sophia followed my gaze to the animals' unblinking glass eyes. "I've been trying to get Dad to give those away. Aren't they horrible?"

We found the clothes on some shelves under the monkey—ten or twelve cardboard boxes full of everything from baby clothes to a wedding dress from the eighties. There were three large boxes labeled "Grant" which contained torn-up jeans, T-shirts from rock concerts, and a pair of gym shorts from Bear Valley High. I grabbed a couple of the T-shirts.

Sophia giggled. "My mom bought these for Grant because she wanted him to be more popular."

I already knew the rest of the story. I held a T-shirt up in front of me. It looked brand new. "Let me guess. He refused to wear them."

"How did you know?"

"My brothers would do the same thing." Come to think of it, so would I. What was friendship worth if you couldn't be authentic?

Sophia found a box at the back of a shelf and pulled it out. The top was covered with a thick layer of dust. "This is the box I was thinking of. I used to play dress up with the clothes in here. Some of the things are really pretty."

"This isn't your mom's stuff, is it?" I asked, but opening the lid, I could see I didn't need to ask. This stuff went way past the nineties and eighties. This couldn't have been stuff from her mother. This was stuff from her grandmother at least.

"No. My mom's stuff is still in her closet. Remind me, and I'll show it to you later."

No way was I going anywhere near Mrs. Tilney's closet, not when her ex-husband was anywhere nearby. "Oh ... okay."

I held up a cute seersucker sundress to myself. It was marked as a size eight, which, in today's sizes would have been a perfect fit, but from what I knew about vanity sizing, it would be at least two sizes too small. Looking at it next to my body, it was clear there was no hope. "On second thought, I think I'll stick with Grant's old gym shorts and T-shirts."

I dug through that box until I'd found three T-shirts that looked to be my size and two pairs of shorts.

I didn't find anything else that fit, but I did find a cute little black sequined purse. "Do you think your dad would mind if I used this purse?"

Sophia replaced the box of vintage dresses on the shelf. "He won't even notice."

"Mine was stolen—and then lost, so I need a purse, but everything inside was stolen too, so what's the point? I have no wallet, no phone, no makeup, no keys."

Sophia flapped her hand at me. "Keep it. You'll find something to put in it."

I put the strap over my shoulder. "Are you sure it's not a family heirloom?"

"It's not, but even if it were, I'd still want you to have it. You're part of our family this week." She paused, a funny smile on her face. "I probably shouldn't tell you this, but Grant has never brought any of his girlfriends home to visit. You're the first."

I worked the clasp on the purse, not daring to return her smile. I really hoped Grant's bringing me here meant something, but I knew better. "He only brought me here because I needed a place to hide."

She leaned on one of the chest freezers. "It's hard to explain, but there's just something more natural about your relationship with him. He's more himself when he's with you. Trust me. I'm his sister. I think you two have a future together."

Maybe she was right. I could see Grant and me dating after all this was through, if all this crime stuff could get resolved. Things did seem natural when we were together.

I folded and stacked the clothes I'd chosen on top of the freezer, and then we put all the other clothes back into the boxes. I'd been too suspicious about Mr. Tilney. Being out in his garage helped me feel like the Tilneys were a normal, rural family— except for all the taxidermy, of course, and Sophia's isolation. My parents had the same type of system in our garage, storing hand-me-downs for the younger siblings, as well as food in the chest freezers. Mom was always asking us to go out to the freezer to get food for dinner, and Mr. Tilney was probably the same way. "Should we bring something in from the freezer since we're out here?" I asked, patting the top of the freezer. Since Mr. Tilney didn't like to hunt anymore, he probably bought a side of beef every year.

She shook her head. "Oh, we haven't used those since I was a little kid. We have a big freezer inside the house."

But I could hear a faint hum coming from them, and they were both plugged in. "It looks like they're still running."

"Dad probably just keeps them going in case the inside freezers get too full." She made an effort to lift the lid, but it didn't budge. "They're locked for safety, but I don't think there's anything inside."

Sophia walked out of the garage, but I didn't move. It didn't make sense that Mr. Tilney would keep his freezers running if there wasn't any food in them. Perhaps, there was something in them other than food—something he felt he had to lock safely away. Something he had to keep secret—like a body.

I shuddered. No, it couldn't be that. There was probably a much more sensible explanation.

CHAPTER 15

One of the worst things about not having a phone was that I never knew what time it was. I had to constantly ask Sophia, or estimate how much time had passed since Grant had left. When I thought it was eleven o'clock, Sophia would tell me it was only ten. When I thought it was twelve, she would tell me it was only eleven thirty. The day slogged along like that as we first went for a run, played with Slurpee, and then trained him to shake. "Do you like to play checkers?" she asked.

It wasn't my favorite game, but what else was there to do? "Sure."

So we played checkers in the living room. Then we ate tuna fish sandwiches in the kitchen for lunch. "Don't you need to do your schoolwork?" I asked Sophia after we'd washed the dishes.

She bit her lip and glanced toward her laptop. "Yeah. I probably should."

"I'll just entertain myself for a while," I said. "I'll be fine."

"Are you sure?" she asked.

The last thing I wanted was for her to get a failing grade because of me. "Oh, yeah," I said. "I should probably take a nap anyway. I haven't gotten much sleep in the last few days."

"And we woke you up early this morning."

Which was totally worth it. I needed to say goodbye to Grant. "That's okay. I'm a good napper. Unless you need me to do anything around the house?"

She eyed the bag of dog food in the corner of the kitchen. "Actually, do you mind taking that big bag of dog food to the garage?" We had filled a canister with Slurpee's food earlier, and there were still about ten pounds in the bag

I walked over and picked it up. "I'd be happy to."

"Here's the key," Sophia said, handing me a ring of keys and pointing out a square one for the garage.

Walking out the backdoor, I scanned my surroundings. There were plenty of places for people to hide in the gardens and woods that surrounded the estate. My kidnappers could be watching me right at that moment. But I couldn't think that way. Grant had promised I was safe here. Still, I hurried as fast as I could to the garage.

My kidnappers had to suspect Grant was hiding me. They knew I'd met him at the diner twice. Yes, they'd searched his truck, and Grant thought that threw them off our trail. But what if it hadn't? What if they'd seen me and had secretly followed us here?

With those thoughts, I unlocked the door to the garage, stepped inside, and locked the door behind me. I turned on the lights and stood still a moment, making sure that no one was lurking anywhere behind a shelf or box. The taxidermy still seemed the same—all the animals staring blankly out of their glass eyes.

I placed the bag of dog food down and sank to the floor beside it. I needed to gather my courage before I went back outside.

I wasn't going to think about those chest freezers. I didn't even want to look at them, but I couldn't help it. Why were they still running if the Tilneys never used them?

I got up from the floor and walked over to them again. That's when I noticed that the lock on one of the freezers had been replaced with a heavy-duty brass lock. Goosebumps prickled my skin. It wasn't like the simple locks we had at home on our freezers—the kind I could open with a paperclip. No, this one demanded its own key.

This was exactly the type of freezer a murderer would use to hide a body.

I let my mind wander back to the story Sophia told me about her mother's last night at the house. Mr. and Mrs. Tilney had yelled at each other. Perhaps Mr. Tilney had hit his wife. Perhaps he'd hit her hard enough that she'd died—I'd heard of such things happening. In a panic, Mr. Tilney had hidden her body in the chest freezer and told the kids she left.

It explained why he would keep the freezer running all these years.

But the whole idea of it was also ridiculous. Mr. Tilney was cranky, but he wasn't a murderer. Grant had told me I could trust him, and there was probably a simple explanation for the high-security lock. In fact, I might be able to open it with one of the keys on the key ring Sophia gave me.

I was standing there, looking for a matching key, when I heard the side door open, and in walked Mr. Tilney.

It felt like my stomach had jumped up into my throat. I wanted to scream. But I couldn't. I just froze there, the keys jangling in my hand.

He had caught me. Now what would he do?

"Good afternoon," he said, staring at me.

I gulped, trying to find my voice. He was blocking my only exit. I couldn't run. I just had to pretend I wasn't scared of him at all, and that I didn't suspect he kept a body in the chest freezer beside me. "Good afternoon," I croaked. My voice came out so quiet, he probably couldn't hear what I said. "I was just finding a place for that bag of dog food." I pointed to where I'd left it on the floor.

"I'm headed off to town," he said, pressing a button to open the large garage door behind the luxury sedan. He didn't seem at all concerned that I was standing near his freezer.

I gulped. "Oh. Have a nice drive."

He opened the driver's side door, got in, and backed out of the driveway. The garage door closed again, leaving me alone with the two chest freezers.

What was I thinking? Grant's dad wasn't a murderer. He was just a little standoffish.

I needed sleep.

I peeked out the side door. After looking around, I ran up the stairs to my guest room, shutting the door and locking it behind me. All the while, I told myself to stop overreacting. The freezer was probably full of old popsicles, and kidnappers weren't hiding in the woods.

Just in case there was someone watching me, though, I closed the shades on all the windows and turned off the lights.

Peering through the gap at the side of the window shade nearest the door, I could see nothing but a chipmunk and two squirrels.

I needed to find the silver lining in my situation. Staying here in Northanger wasn't so bad. I'd anticipated a spring break, trying to figure out what kind of excitement I could drum up around the farm, so I could increase my vlog audience past fourteen people. It should have been a relief to get away from the farm, where the most exciting thing to do was play Candy Land with my youngest sister or drive fifty miles to the community college for my advanced calculus class.

At home, I almost never encountered a guy in his twenties. Even more rarely did I meet someone so kind with as nice a personality as Grant's. Now I was the oldest child left at home, the only one who hadn't managed to get a scholarship, and so I was roughing it, working at the town hall during the day with coworkers who were over the age of seventy—and attending the community college in the evenings. My life was probably even more boring than the life of a truck driver, so, though I had hated being kidnapped, I counted my blessings that I was at least out of my little country town for a few days.

I turned on the TV, but I kept the volume low, so I would hear any footsteps on the stairs coming up to my room. I flipped back and forth between the History Channel and the Cooking Channel, sometimes choosing to watch the commercials rather than the actual shows. Both channels were just what I needed to help myself relax and fall asleep, but I couldn't stop watching and listening for footsteps on the stairs.

I must have finally nodded off because the next thing I knew, I was at home at my parents' farm lying in bed, and my younger sister was pounding on my door. "Eva?" she yelled. "Are you okay?" Probably she was trying to get me up for breakfast. Only, I wasn't hungry.

"Go away," I muttered. "I'm tired." It was so comfortable, lying there. I hadn't slept so well in weeks.

But how had I gotten home? My eyes fluttered open, and after a moment's disorientation, I realized I was still in my guest room over the Tilney's garage.

116

"Eva?" someone yelled from the other side of the door. It was Sophia's voice.

"I'm coming," My voice came out hoarse, the way it often does in the morning, especially when someone calls me on the phone at nine a.m. and I have to pretend I'm a responsible farmer, and I haven't been asleep.

When I finally heaved myself off the sofa and opened the door, Sophia held her phone out to me. "Grant wants to talk to you."

I took the phone. "Hey," I said as Sophia pivoted and headed down the stairs.

"Hey yourself," Grant answered. "How are things going?"

"Fine," I said. I wasn't about to mention any of my worries about kidnappers or freezers. "Sophia's a lot of fun. So where are you exactly?"

"In Northern Oklahoma, at Granny Annie's."

"Granny Annie's?" I asked. He hadn't told me anything about a grandmother.

"You've never heard of Granny Annie's? It's a chain of truck stops all across the Midwest. I try to stop at every one on my route. Their food is good, and it's not too expensive."

"Oh," I said, letting the word hang in the air for a while. "I wish I could've gone along to keep you company. Trucking seems like it must be boring."

"That's why it's not my choice for a permanent career."

I never had bothered to figure out why he was in trucking. The waitress had said it was his family's business, but perhaps he'd told her that to cover up his double agent thing.

"Hey," he said, "my dad's heading into town and I thought maybe it'd be a good idea to get you some new clothes."

How could that be a good idea? Don't get me wrong. I loved the idea of new clothes. What I didn't love was having Grant's dad buy them. "Oh, I'm getting by okay. Sophia helped me find some of your old rock concert T-shirts."

What came through the phone sounded almost like a snort. "You're welcome to them, but I'd still like Dad to pick up a few things for you. What size should I tell him to get you."

117

Size? As if I were a man and could simply buy a size off the rack without trying anything on. "I'm usually an eight," I said, "but I'm not sure this is a great idea. What kind of store is he going to?"

"He was thinking of going to the ranch store."

"So I'll be wearing cowgirl clothes?"

He laughed. "The more you look like a cowgirl, the better."

"Because you find that attractive?" I'd thought he liked my vintage clothes.

"Don't start thinking I have a cowgirl fetish. I want you to wear cowgirl clothes so you'll blend in. If someone sees you walking around the yard with Sophia, I want them to think you're just a girl from the next town over."

It was actually a good idea: another disguise. Why hadn't I thought of that? Maybe because I'd been spending so much of my mental energy worrying about kidnappers in the woods and a body in the freezer. "Hey, I was going to ask you—whatever happened to your mom? Does she live around here?"

It was like we'd been disconnected. He didn't say anything for the longest time.

"Are you still there?" I asked.

"Yeah," he said, "I'm still here … I just had someone pull in front of me. I had to slam on the brakes." Was he telling the truth, or just trying to make an excuse for his silence?

"People need to learn how to drive around trucks," I said, repeating a line I'd often heard my father say.

"You can say that again. So what have you and Sophia been doing?" It sounded like he was trying to change the subject.

Did I dare ask him about his mom again? Yes, I did. "Well, for one thing, we talked about your mom. Sophia says she hasn't heard from her since your parents divorced. I was just wondering why that is."

"Dad didn't think a toxic relationship would be good for us, so that was part of the divorce agreement. Mom got plenty of money, and Dad got to protect our mental health."

I couldn't imagine Mr. Tilney being all that concerned about mental health.

"So what else did you do today?" Grant asked.

I told him about playing with the dog, watching the movie, and walking out to the creek.

"The early morning is the best time to explore Northanger," he said. "Sometimes you might see deer or foxes. Dad's better at finding them than Sophia and I are. You should ask him to take a walk with you tonight."

"Um. Okay." There was no way I was asking his father to go on a walk with me—even if he might help me find a deer or fox. "So, it'll probably be two or three more days until you're back?"

"More like five or six—depending. You can call me on Sophia's phone anytime."

Five or six days! "My spring break will be over by then. I'll hardly have any time to be with you before I go home."

"I'm not sure it'll be safe for you to go home even then." His words came slowly, as if he might be afraid of my reaction. "I might need a couple more days to work things out."

He needed more time to work things out? I wanted to ask what kinds of things he needed to work out, but I was fed up with all the mystery. This needed to end. "I can't afford to miss my classes next week. I'm barely passing advanced calculus."

"None of that will matter if you're dead." He said it almost in a whisper.

The tightness in my chest returned. I couldn't respond. He was right. I was in serious danger, and he probably was too. I couldn't rush this. If I had to retake my classes, I probably could. These would definitely be considered extenuating circumstances, and people had gotten permission to repeat a semester for less than this. The community college would understand.

"I'll try to call later tonight. Bye."

"Bye," I said.

There was such a crazy mix of feelings inside me. For one thing, I liked Grant. It was exciting to become more and more a part of his life. On the other hand, I had to worry about whether I'd actually survive to have a life with him. And if he really was a double agent, was it even possible to have a life with him? Could

119

I trust him that all this danger would come to an end in a few more days?

I stared at the phone as my heart raced. I was way too stressed out. What did I do at home to relieve my stress? I'd already watched a movie, played with a dog, and gone on a walk. The only other thing I could think of was an organizing project. When I got super stressed, I'd organize my room or another area of our home. It gave me a sense of relief and satisfaction to clean things out, to complete a big project.

I opened the door and glanced down the stairway. Sophia must have gone back in the house. She had plenty of projects—between her schoolwork, the yard, and the house, I was sure she could find something I could do.

I found her back in the living room, where I'd left her. She was typing away on her laptop.

"Is there anything I can do to help around the house?"

"Um." Sophia didn't look up.

"Something to keep my mind off my stress. I thought you might be able to help me with that since you seem to have way more projects going on than I do."

She stopped, still staring at her screen. "Sorry. I was focused on this essay. What did you say again?"

"I was wondering if I could help clean out a closet or an old shed—I'll do anything really." I was hoping it would be a project that could help me understand Grant's family a little better. "I'm really good with video editing if you have any old videos you need to preserve."

Sophia tipped her head to the side. "I guess you could help weed the garden if you like. I've been ignoring it terribly because of my classes."

It wasn't quite the project I was hoping for, but perhaps it would help her trust me with something closer to her heart.

Sophia came out to the garden with me. "I need a break from studying anyway," she said.

I had never seen a garden with so few weeds. The only ones we found were just starting to peek through the earth. "I think you have the cutest weeds I've ever seen," I said.

120

"Yes, but they grow up to be monsters," she said, "I promise."

"Isn't that the way it always is? Everyone is cute as a baby? Did your high school do that thing at graduation where they show each person's baby picture on the big screen while they go up to get their diploma?"

Sophia shrugged. "No, but that might be because I was homeschooled."

"Oh." Knowing all I knew about her father, I should have guessed she was homeschooled. "Well, it just always surprised me that everyone, no matter what they looked like as teenagers, had been a beautiful baby."

"I suppose so," she said, "I don't remember ever seeing my baby pictures."

"But—" I began, thinking of the pictures on the wall in the living room. There was one of Grant as a toddler, but I couldn't remember any baby pictures.

Sophia shoved the pile of weeds down deeper into her compost bucket. "That's one of the things about being raised by your dad. They don't think about pictures as much as mothers."

That wasn't true in my own family. My dad loved to take pictures as much as my mom, but this was the Tilneys we were talking about. I didn't want to make Sophia feel bad by telling her that.

"I think Dad doesn't like to look at old pictures," she added. "It's too emotional for him, knowing how much we've lost."

"I guess that would be hard." I'd heard people were like that after a death sometimes, even more so after a divorce, but wouldn't he still want to see pictures of Sophia and Grant as babies?

"Sometimes I am curious to see the old pictures," Sophia said. "I once asked Dad if I could look at them."

"What did he say?"

"He said they're on one of his old computers, and he can't remember where he put it." She reached for a dandelion that had

121

found its way among her flowers, yanking it out by the root. "Take that!"

It seemed like by now, Sophia should have been able to find an old computer that was stored somewhere around the house. Surely, with all the time she spent at home, she could have found it. "Have you looked for the old computer?" I asked.

She shook her head. "Not really. He has about twenty of them lying here and there around the house, and they're all password protected. Even if we did find the right machine, Dad's probably forgotten the password."

I sometimes wondered at Sophia's passivity. If my pictures were hidden away on one of my dad's old computers, I would have found a way to get past the password by now. Yet, she seemed perfectly content to spend her days weeding the gardens and studying online. Had she ever considered running away? I'd have to ask her about it. Maybe not today, but later on before I left.

We worked in the garden for another hour before Mr. Tilney came home, a large bag in one hand and a pizza box in the other. "I brought dinner from town. Come inside to eat before it gets cold."

We dusted off our hands and followed Mr. Tilney into the house.

"The pizza at Antonio's is the best," Sophia said in a cheerful tone. "What kind did you get, Dad?"

"Sausage and mushroom."

Of course it would have to be mushroom. I'd hated them since I saw a *Murder She Wrote* episode where the victim died from poisoned mushrooms. Even so, I followed Mr. Tilney into the kitchen, washed my hands, and sat down at the table.

Sophia passed out plates while Mr. Tilney spread a napkin on his lap. "You're probably used to better food than this," he said. "Doesn't your father's company produce an organic food label?"

"Um. Yes." I had no idea how he'd found out that our family grew organic peaches. Maybe Grant had told him. "But I'm okay eating non-organic. I do it all the time when I'm not at home."

As Sophia sat down beside me, I reached for her hand, preparing to say grace—an old habit from home. They both bit into the pizza instead. I could do this. I could pretend I didn't need to say grace, and that mushrooms didn't bother me. I brought a slice to my lips and took a bite.

I had to admit, it was good pizza—I barely noticed the mushroom taste.

Mr. Tilney held up a finger. "I almost forgot. Grant told me to get you some cowgirl clothes, but they didn't have anything like that at WalMart."

He walked to the other room and came back carrying a black, long-sleeve maxi dress on a hanger. I was going to look like an Amish woman in mourning—if that was even a thing.

"What do you think?" he asked, turning the dress so I could see that the back zipped all the way up to my neck.

I pasted on a smile. "That looks fabulous. It'll be a perfect disguise." I could put my hair up in a tight bun to complete the ensemble.

Mr. Tilney laid the dress over a chair next to me and sat back down at the table. "You'll notice I'm old fashioned. I don't go for these miniskirts, low cut blouses, or torn-up jeans, and this was the only item in the store that fit the bill."

"Thank you, sir. I'm glad I won't have to go around the house looking like—" I was going to say a hillbilly slut, but I decided that might not qualify as polite conversation. "—um, a white trash diva."

Mr. Tilney didn't seem offended at all. "In this family, we prefer women who are well-bred and modest. Of course, that's a mighty tall order nowadays." I pressed my lips together to keep from responding. He might not think I was good enough for his son, but he didn't have to insult my breeding. He went on, oblivious to my feelings. "It's just as hard to find a woman who knows how to handle money. Most women aren't fit to handle a family fortune. They're more likely to be money grubbers."

I gritted my teeth. How snobby could a guy get? His son was a truck driver, and yet he spoke as if Grant were Bill Gates or the Prince of England. "So you want your son to marry someone who's good at managing your trucking business?" I asked, barely keeping the anger from my voice.

"My business is not trucking," he said, looking down his nose at me.

I'd taken a bite just at the wrong time, and my mouth was still full. I hurried to gulp my food down. "Oh, yes, I keep forgetting."

"I'm a real estate investor," he continued. "My son is a lawyer."

I took a swig of my drink to get that bite of pizza down my throat. How was I going to get through another six days of this?

CHAPTER 16

Over the next few days at the Tilney house, I managed to fall into a routine: breakfast at sunrise, a walk into the woods, a movie while Sophia did homework, a run with the dog, and then lunch, followed by one of the projects Sophia and Mr. Tilney reluctantly agreed to let me do.

First, I washed the outside of all the windows, which took some skill, considering I had to lean a twenty-foot extension ladder against the house and then climb it in my Amish-style mourning dress—all while carrying a bucket in one hand. The first time I got up to the second floor, the skirt of my dress tangled around my legs, and it took me a good five minutes to climb down. I'm not sure if Amish women ever climb extension ladders, but after my experience, I'd recommend they steer clear. Once I got my feet on the ground, I headed back to my room, where I changed into one of Grant's old T-shirts and shorts. Riding in an ambulance wasn't my idea of blending into the community.

The next day, I donned another T-shirt to sweep out the garage and the sheds. Then I spent the next two days caring for trees and shrubs, also in a T-shirt. I was an expert at trees, after all, having grown up on an orchard.

I have to confess, though, I was disappointed that Mr. Tilney wouldn't allow me more indoor chores, where I could explore the nooks and crannies of the house. I was especially curious about the old computer that held all of Sophia's baby pictures. It would be a shame to lose those pictures forever. I promised myself that the next time Grant called, I'd ask him if he knew anything about the computer. It was the least I could do for Sophia after all she'd done to welcome me into her home.

Grant's calls came at the most unexpected times, and this one came right after I'd climbed to the top of the biggest peach tree and perched myself on a sturdy branch, ready to thin peaches from its branches. Sophia had to toss me the phone from down below.

"So what are you up to today?" Grant asked when I answered.

"Funny you should ask," I said, climbing down one branch at a time.

"Have you decided to replace the shingles on that old shed?" I could tell by the tone of his voice that he was teasing about the shed. He already thought I was doing too much, but I'd assured him that this was exactly what I needed.

I jumped down from the bottom branch. "I'm thinning peaches. You're going to have the best crop you can imagine this year."

"I wish you were relaxing instead."

I plucked a few baby peaches from the grass and threw them into a bucket. "But this helps me relax. Speaking of which—for my next project, I want to help Sophia find her baby pictures. They're on an old computer, and your dad can't remember where it is. Do you know?"

There was a pause on the other end. "No."

"Well, do you have any guesses?"

"No, and I wouldn't go looking for it either."

"Why not?"

"Just trust me."

At the sound of those words, it was as if a hundred-foot damn cracked open, and all my anger burst free. Trust him. Again. What did Sophia's baby pictures have to do with my kidnapping or his secret mission? Probably nothing. Grant just had to keep yet another secret from me. There was no other explanation. "How long do you expect me to trust you?" I asked, my voice betraying my rage. "Or am I supposed to live out the rest of my life as a hermit like your sister."

This time his answer came faster. "Sophia isn't a hermit."

Yes, I could have chosen a better word to describe Sophia than hermit. I hadn't meant to get her involved. It wasn't her fault her brother kept so many secrets. "Okay, then, maybe it's more accurate to call her a prisoner. That's what she is. She hasn't spent a single night away from you or your father, has she?"

I could hear him groan on the other end. "You don't understand, Eva."

"No, I don't," I said, my volume rising. "That's the whole problem. Everything is a secret. How could I understand anything that's going on?"

Silence hung between us before Grant finally spoke again. "This isn't a movie. This is real life, Eva. In real life, it's better if you don't know everything. It keeps you out of trouble."

Instead of responding to my concern, he'd insulted me. "Can't you at least try to understand how frustrating it is for me to live in confusion like this?" I'd trusted him for almost a week now, and every day that passed, I had more and more questions.

"Please don't go looking for that computer." He sounded just like his father. "I know it seems like a good idea, but it would do much more harm than good."

My breath caught. Did he think I was going to look for something on the computer other than pictures? "I was only trying to help Sophia. I wasn't planning to violate anyone's privacy."

"I'll see you tomorrow," he said, his voice stiff. "Hopefully, I can get things worked out, so you can go home after that."

So he wanted to send me home. He wanted to be done with me. "I'm sorry, Grant," I said, but he had already hung up. It was our first fight, and in a way, it was a relief. I was so sick of secrets and hiding. If that's the way a relationship with Grant was going to be, I was better off without him. It sounded like he felt the same way about me too.

CHAPTER 17

A knock sounded in the pitch black. At first, I thought it was my imagination. Who would be knocking so late at night? Then it happened again—three loud knocks, just like the first time. The clock on my nightstand said two a. m. Was something wrong? While Slurpee ran to the door, his tail wagging, I turned on the lights and fumbled to unlock the door. Sophia stepped inside. "I'm really sorry to wake you up," she said. Her eyes were wide, her hair a tangled mess, her hands gripped in front of her.

"What's wrong?" I asked. Had something happened to Grant? I was still mad at him for keeping so many secrets, but underneath it all, I cared about him more than I'd cared for any other man.

She raked her hand through her hair. "You're so sweet, Eva, which makes this even harder for me."

I bit my lip. Maybe it was about Grant. Did it have something to do with our fight over the phone? "Just tell me what's wrong. I can handle it." I grabbed onto a chair and sat down just in case I really couldn't handle it. Grant had become my only lifeline through this crisis. I was also hoping to continue our relationship after this whole mess was over. That was the one thing that kept me from completely freaking out. What would I do if something happened to Grant?

Sophia dragged a chair over to sit beside me. She clasped my hands in hers. "Dad told me he's going to call the police to come get you in the morning. He doesn't know I'm here right now, but I couldn't let it happen. I wanted to warn you."

"He's going to call the police," I repeated, still trying to process her words. Grant had told me to stay here. He'd said it was the only place where I would be safe.

This had to be about my conversation with Grant. It was the only reason that made any sense. "Did Grant tell him I was looking for his old computer? I was only trying to help you find your baby pictures." If that's all it was, I could explain everything to Mr. Tilney.

She shook her head. "I think it had to do with a video he saw." She glanced around at my things. "We have to hurry. I don't want Dad to know I'm here."

"What video did he see?" I asked. It was probably the security camera footage of me hitting Ingrid over the head, but there were probably hundreds of ways my vlogs could have offended him. It could have been my political views, a dress he didn't like, something I'd said about fair trade practices, or who knows what else? I'd made hundreds of vlogs.

Sophia pulled out her phone. "There's actually more than one. I can find them while you pack." She spoke with certainty, as if there was nothing I could do to change her father's mind.

I gulped. This was it, then. I had no choice but to leave. But where could I go? I didn't know anyone in Oklahoma, and I had no way to get home. "Are you sure it wouldn't be better to stay and wait for the police to come?" I asked.

"Hold on," she said, staring down at her phone. "Once you see these videos, you'll understand. I wish the internet connection wasn't so slow out here."

"I bet I know which one," I said, holding out my hand for her phone. She gave it to me, and I quickly found the video of me hitting Ingrid over the head. "That woman is the one who kidnapped me. The only reason I hit her was because I was afraid she was going to kidnap me again, and I took the purse because it was mine. She took it from me. My brother's roommate was there. He can verify my story."

"No," Sophia said, shaking her head and taking her phone back. "that wasn't the one. We all saw that one before you got here." She continued scrolling down through the feed. "It's one with that guy Clayton Thorpe. He made a few videos, in which he defended your actions. But yesterday, he published one that said he's been mistaken all along" She paused to click on a link. "Here it is."

The video played while I bent over her phone to watch. "Eva Morland deceived me," Clayton said, speaking into the camera. "She led me to believe that she was a sweet girl from a

129

wealthy family, but everything she said was a lie. She was just using me and my good name to—"

"A wealthy girl? I never said anything like that." I balled my hands into fists, wishing I could punch him in the throat.

Sophia paused the video. "He says you were pretending to be a victim so that you could build your vlogging platform and get more attention. He accused you of lying about owning Morland Organics."

I slapped my hand over my mouth, remembering my conversation with Mr. Tilney about my family's organic farm. He must have thought we owned *the* Morland Organics. My family often joked about running Morland Organics, but no one in our little farm town would ever mistake us for that family. "I never told Clayton we owned Morland Organics. He must have just assumed." To think that I ever agreed to go to dinner with that guy! What a jerk.

Sophia fumbled in her pockets, taking out a key and twisting it in her fingers. "Clayton also said you'd cheated him out of a few thousand dollars."

"What?" I clutched at the collar of my pajamas. "I never took his money! I was only with him for one afternoon. Of all the idiotic … You don't believe him, do you?"

Sophia heaved a sigh. "No, but what does it matter what I think? Dad is afraid you're dishonest, and you're after Grant's money. I tried to call Grant about it, but he turns his phone off when he goes to sleep. It probably wouldn't have made a difference anyway. Dad thinks you've tricked Grant the way you tricked Clayton." She handed me the key. "I want you to take my car. It's not much, but it has a full tank of gas. It's the old sedan in the garage."

"I can't take your car." I was sure that would make Mr. Tilney even madder at me.

Sophia shrugged. "You have no other way to get home."

I hated to tell her this, but a tank of gas wouldn't get me home—I lived all the way down in the South of Texas—and I had no money. Still, it was better than nothing. A car could get me far enough to call home for help.

Sophia glanced over at the T-shirts I had stacked on top of the dresser. "I'll help you pack."

"Your dad will think I stole the clothes and your car." That was all I needed—to be accused of stealing from Mr. Tilney on top of everything else.

I tried to give her back the key, but she folded her arms, shaking her head. "I'm loaning it to you. That's what I'm going to tell Dad when he sees it's gone." She pulled a few granola bars from her pocket and handed them to me. Then she walked over to the window and looked out, probably worried that her dad might be watching.

For about the hundredth time, I wondered why she put up with her dad. "Did it ever occur to you that your father might be …" I didn't want to say abusive, so I said, "restrictive?"

She rifled through the top drawer of the dresser, pulled out a canvas bag and handed it to me. "You can use this to pack your things … It has occurred to me that Dad's restrictive. I can't tell you how many times I've talked to Grant about that, but Grant says that's what's best for me right now."

"That's practically the same thing Grant said to me about staying here in Northanger—that I would be safe." I couldn't care less that I sounded angry. All it took was two videos, and he was calling the cops on me.

I gathered up my little stack of clothes and walked down the stairs with Sophia. My mind raced as she whispered the directions that would take me to the nearest town, but I couldn't process much of it. "Once you get to town," she said, "you can take the freeway home. Please text me when you get there." Then she seemed to remember I didn't have a phone. "Here." She opened the glove compartment, ripped a sheet of paper from the car manual and wrote her number on it. "I'm not supposed to keep in touch with you, but one text won't hurt."

She wasn't supposed to keep in touch with me? It was one more odd request on top of all the others her father had made.

She gave me a hug. "The important thing is that you're innocent. The police will figure that out eventually. I wish I could

131

help you more." She pulled back. "Oh, I forgot." She pulled a credit card from her back pocket.

I hesitated. "I can't take this, Sophia, after all the other things you've done for me."

"You'll never make it on just one tank," she said.

It was true. I had to take it. Not that I knew where I was going, but it would be nice to have the option of driving all the way home. The only problem was that I'd never driven far without a phone to help me figure out directions. "Which direction did you say was the closest town?"

She pointed to the right. "It's about forty-five minutes that way. I'm so sorry I can't help you anymore, Eva." She hugged me again.

After Sophia opened the garage door, I said goodbye to Slurpee and got inside the old sedan. My parents had a car similar to it when I was younger, but I'd never driven it. Mashing my foot down on the brake, I took the car out of park. Then, easing off the brake, I backed the car out until I could feel the crunch of gravel beneath the tires. After turning the car back toward the driveway, I shifted into drive and lightly pressed the gas. The car zoomed forward, much faster than I'd intended to go. Following its lead, I roared forward into the uncertainty, my high beams piercing the pitch black.

CHAPTER 18

I had no idea where I was going as I drove away from the Tilney Estate. All I knew was that I needed to get to the closest town. From there, I didn't have much choice but to go home ... unless I could figure out how to meet back up with Grant.

Just a few hours earlier, I'd thought that Grant and I were finished. Yes, I was sick of all the secrets, but he was the only one who'd at least given me a hint about the secrets. He understood my situation and would know what to do. So what if he was still mad at me? He'd gotten me into this mess in the first place. Why hadn't I thought to ask Sophia for his phone number before I left?

If only I knew the route Grant was taking and I could somehow catch him along the road. He was due home later that day, and he was coming from South Dakota—that would be a north-west direction. Beyond that I didn't know much, except that he always stopped at Granny Annie's truck stops. Maybe I could wait for him at the closest one to home? All I had to do was find out where that was and wait there. Since I had no phone, that wouldn't be as easy as it normally would be. I'd have to stop and ask directions.

When I arrived at the town forty-five minutes later, everything was closed—just as it would be in the town near our farm in Texas. A sign on the gas station said they would open at eight. The clock on the dashboard read two thirty. I pulled over to the side of the road and cracked the window, hoping that despite my nerves, I could maybe get some sleep before morning. In the distance, lightning lit the sky with thunder following close after. Breathing in, I caught a whiff of manure. Not that I'd ever particularly enjoyed the smell of manure, but it did make me feel at home. All it needed was a hint of skunk.

Sitting there, counting the seconds between the lightning and thunder, I wondered about what Grant had said—that I shouldn't leave his Dad's house because it was the only place I was safe. Did that mean I wasn't safe out here? Could my kidnappers find me here? I also worried a little about Mr. Tilney.

What if he'd found out I had Sophia's car? Would he come looking for me? Then what would I do? I started the car again, this time driving it off the main road and following a few small roads until I found a tiny dirt road that ran behind a church. Making sure no one had followed me, I parked the car behind a hedge.

I'd never been so happy for the crack of lightning, growing ever close. Within minutes, a drenching rain enveloped the car, providing both obscurity from passersby and the perfect white noise to lull me to sleep.

I dreamed that I was back with Mrs. Garland in the trailer. She had tied me to a chair and poured fire starter on me. Just as she was about to drop the match, I woke with a start, my heart racing.

I gripped the steering wheel in front of me. The rain had died down. Turning my head in all directions, I couldn't see anyone around me. The car doors were locked. I was perfectly safe parked behind the little church. Still, I wanted to turn the key, press the gas pedal to the floor, and peel out of that dark town as fast as I could.

The problem was that I didn't know where to go.

I pulled my arms up into the sleeves of my T-shirt, trying to fight off the shivers. I didn't dare waste gas by turning on the heater. *You're going to be fine, Eva. No one's going to come looking for you here.*

It took me at least an hour to fall asleep again, but it was like that one time in high school when we drove on the bus overnight to Disneyworld. I woke over and over again until the sun peeked over the horizon.

At 7:45 a.m., I snuck out of the car and wandered down the little road, keeping in the shadows of trees and shrubs.

The town consisted of a tiny main street—two big churches with steeples, a high school and an elementary school. There was a little park with a couple of picnic tables and a statue of a man on a horse. I saw a woman hauling her dirty clothes into the laundromat, but the hair salon and insurance agency weren't yet open.

134

I lingered beside the gas station until a pickup truck pulled into the parking lot, and a gray-haired man in a jumpsuit got out.

I didn't even wait for him to unlock the front door. I went right up to him as he fumbled with his keys. "Excuse me, sir. Can you tell me how to get to the closest Granny Annie's?"

"Granny Annie's?" He closed one eye and smooshed his lips together. "Sorry ma'am. I don't know." He twisted the key in the lock and pushed open the glass door to the office.

I followed him inside, my hands clasped as if in prayer. "Do you think you could look it up for me? I've lost my phone, and I could really use your help? I'm kind of desperate."

He shrugged and handed me his phone. "You're welcome to use my phone for a minute. I'm no good at technology."

I could barely refrain from hugging him before I took the phone. "Oh, thank you."

He walked back behind the little counter and plopped into his desk chair. "It's no problem."

I put Granny Annie's into the search bar. When the results came up, I punched my hand into the air. "Yes!" There were two in Oklahoma, one in Northwestern Oklahoma and the other in Northeastern. Having already decided Grant would be coming from the West, I picked the northwestern one and drew myself a map on a scrap of paper. It would likely take all the gas in the tank to get there. Hopefully, Mr. Tilney hadn't found out about Sophia giving me her credit card.

Realizing I'd have to hurry, I returned the man's phone and ran back to Sophia's car. My brothers were constantly reminding me how bad I was at following directions, but this time, there wasn't much that could go wrong. All I had to do was head to the northwest corner of Oklahoma on the biggest roads I could find.

Since I didn't have a license, I did my best to drive at the speed limit although my impatience to arrive at Granny Annie's often made my foot press harder on the gas pedal. I drove four hours to get there, stopping on the way to buy a tank of gas and a loaf of bread with Sophia's credit card.

On the way, I'd seen numerous billboards for Granny Annie's, which featured a little old lady on a rocking chair in front of a white and red house, but the actual place didn't look much like the house on the billboards. It was simply a large gas station that included a row of diesel pumps for trucks. The only similarity was that the outside of the store was decorated with white and red accents. Looking around, I didn't see Grant's truck anywhere. Walking inside, I found the usual convenience store that stocked the bare essentials. Then I caught a glimpse inside the fast food place. Grant was standing right there in his signature blue T-shirt and jeans, grabbing a few napkins from the dispenser. What were the odds I'd find him just now? Fifteen minutes later, and he probably would have been gone. It was the first stroke of luck I'd had in days.

"Grant," I called, my voice just loud enough for him to hear.

His head whipped around, his eyes wide, but he didn't say a thing. It was like he was looking right through me. He must not have expected to find me here, dressed in my disguise of an old T-shirt and shorts. After the night I'd had last night, my hair was also looking a mess.

Maybe it was my imagination, but he gave the slightest shake of his head.

Did he not hear me? I spoke louder this time, stepping out from behind the wall. "Grant, it's me, Eva. I need your help."

That's when I saw the woman with dark hair standing to the left of Grant. She wasn't just any woman, though. She was the same woman I'd met in the trailer, the woman my kidnappers called Mrs. Garland. "What are you—" she said to Grant, but her words dropped off as she focused her gaze on me.

CHAPTER 19

I stood there long enough to see Ronald and the man from the trailer standing behind Mrs. Garland. Grant's face remained a blank slate. He didn't send me the slightest wink.

I'd just interrupted a meeting between him and the bad guys. Now they knew he and I were working together, and since they still thought I was Leslie Kaplan, they would surely figure out that he wasn't really on their side. I'd done something I'd promised never to do—I'd let the bad guys know that he was a double agent. Now they would probably try to kill him. I couldn't live with myself if that happened because of me. And darn it all, despite the fact that his father was a jerk and our last conversation had ended in an argument, I liked him. I had to do something to save him, and I had to do it quickly.

The problem was, all my legs wanted was to run away as fast as they could. And that is exactly what I let them do. Mrs. Garland was no match for my adrenaline-fueled pace. I raced straight to Sophia's car, got in, and locked the doors. I didn't know where I was going. All I knew was I wasn't staying.

I had to do something to save Grant, though, before I left, so I drove in a loop around the parking lot while I thought things through. Could I create a diversion that would allow Grant to escape? Could I call the police to tell them I'd found my kidnapper? Could I run over Mrs. Garland as she walked out of Granny Annie's? I couldn't just leave Grant on his own. I'd ruined his undercover operation, and placed his life in peril.

After two laps around the parking lot, I'd given up hope of finding a reasonable solution. Then I caught a glimpse of a black sedan. I slowed down just enough to see that Ingrid was inside and to read the license plate: Texas 676 CRX. It wasn't the same car he'd used when he'd kidnapped me. Of course, it wouldn't be. After all, that car had been stolen.

I had to act quickly before she noticed me. I drove up beside the row of diesel pumps and found a female trucker, who had just pulled up to her pump. She was a tiny woman with dyed red hair, who, except for the studded collar around her neck, looked like she would have fit in better as a bank teller, but she flashed me a smile, so I spoke, "I was wondering if you could help me with something." I'd always heard truckers would band together to help people out. Now was as good a time as any to see if it was true.

Her forehead crinkled, and she placed her hands on her hips. "Someone bothering you, honey?"

"Someone's bothering my boyfriend. He's a trucker, and he's inside the restaurant." I paused, wondering if I should tell the truth—not that I knew all of it. "He's been working as a double agent with the federal government, and now the criminals have found out about it."

She held up one hand. "You mean they're hauling drugs? Say no more." She snapped her gum and went to talk with the brawny male trucker at the next gas pump, who promptly stopped the pump and approached me.

"What's your boyfriend look like?" he asked.

"He's got dark hair. He's about six feet tall and wearing a blue T-shirt. His name is Grant."

The guy nodded, punching his fist into his hand. "And you say he's gotten into trouble with some drug lords?"

I had to sound confident if this was going to work. "They just found out he's a double agent, and I'm afraid they're going to kill him. I just want to make sure he gets away in his own truck."

By this time, the woman was heading back my way with a couple more guys, and the brawny truck driver called out to them. "We've got a tall guy in a blue T-shirt inside the restaurant." Then he turned to me again. "What do the bad guys look like?"

"There are two women and two men, but the red-haired woman will stand out the most. She's wearing sequins, and she's middle-aged."

He punched his hand again and started walking toward the restaurant. "Let's do this."

"Thank you so much," I said, turning back to Sophia's car.

"You're not going to stick around and help your boyfriend?" the female trucker asked. I could feel the weight of her glare on the back of my neck, but the truth was that I was in as much trouble as Grant was.

If I ever saw Grant again, he was either going to thank me or kill me for getting the truckers involved. I hoped it didn't turn into a fiasco.

I swallowed hard. I might never see him again. I might never know if he got away from Mrs. Garland or if he ever succeeded in his mission or if he would ever forgive me for showing up at Granny Annie's.

As I drove down the freeway, all I could do was pray over and over again that Grant would be safe. This time, I was heading south toward home. I no longer worried about being caught by the police or getting followed by my kidnappers. I just wanted Grant to get away. Now that I was locked in Sophia's car, I would be fine.

I stopped only three times when the gas gauge hit empty to fill up, use the restroom, and buy food. Sophia's credit card worked each time, and I kept the receipts, vowing that I would pay her back for all of it. Sometime after I got home, I'd find a way to get the car back to her, along with her credit card and the money, but I wasn't ever going back to the Tilney Estate. Not after the way Mr. Tilney betrayed me. If it hadn't been for him, I would have never gone to that Granny Annie's and blown Grant's cover.

It was past midnight when I drove down the dirt road to my parent's farm. The lights were all out, which was the way I wanted it. No one needed to know I was home. My plan was to hide out in our old playhouse behind the barn. The kids were too old to use it anymore, so no one would know I was there. The last thing I wanted was for my family members to get in trouble for harboring a fugitive—or whatever I was.

Feeling as empty as the gas tank, I drove the car behind the barn and covered it with some black plastic sheeting. I'd been rejected by the Tilneys, and I couldn't set foot in my own home. A week earlier, Grant had compared me to Grace Kelly, prepped and ready for a date. Now I felt more like the leper in *Ben Hur*.

Trying to distract myself from my worries about Grant, I found a sleeping bag in one of the sheds and had tossed it down on the playhouse floor when the door burst open and a flashlight shone in my face. "Eva! Where have you been?" It was my teenage brother, Damien.

I placed a finger over my mouth. "Shh. You're not supposed to know I'm here."

Then, something happened that I never would have expected from this little brother of mine who hated any form of affection. He rushed right up to me and put his hands on my shoulders. "Do you know how worried we've been?"

For the first time that day, a tear escaped my eye. It had been a long day—a long week—after all, and it was nice to know that someone wanted me around. Yes, I was a criminal. Mr. Tilney thought I was a liar, and Grant probably didn't want to see my face ever again. But Damien still loved me. "You're not supposed to know I'm here," I said. "I don't want you to get in trouble with the police."

"Are you kidding me?" Damien responded, sounding much older than his high school sophomore self. "Mom and Dad will kill me if I don't tell them." With that, he took out his phone and was about to call them, but I pulled it away from him.

"Promise you won't tell them." I clasped my hands in front of me. "It's illegal for them to know I'm out here and not tell the police about it."

"What's wrong with telling the police you're here? You're innocent, aren't you? We thought you were dead, Eva. Talking to the police is way better than being dead."

"Can't we at least wait until morning?" I asked. "I'm really tired."

He stared down at the plywood floor, which from what I remembered, was full of splinters. "You're going to sleep here? On this dirty floor?" He looked up at me. "No way." With that, he slipped back out the door.

I called after him. "Please don't tell them, Damien."

I could hear him running to the house and flinging open the screen door in back. He didn't keep the promise I begged him to keep. "Eva's home! She's okay!" he called. The windows must have been open because I could hear the commotion as the whole family woke.

The lights flashed on in every bedroom, and within a minute, Damien emerged from the house, carrying the mattress from my bed. My parents and siblings followed, carrying pillows, sheets, a chair, and some clothes.

"I told you not to tell them," I said as Damien squeezed my mattress through the door of the playhouse.

My mother hugged me, and I could feel that her face was wet with tears. "We'll pretend we don't know you're hiding here. It'll be okay, sweetie. We're just so happy you're home."

I sat down on my mattress while my little brothers and sisters piled onto me, each vying for a hug. Yes, I was a criminal, but my family still loved me. I might have to go to prison for a while, and the man of my dreams might never forgive me, but I still had things to live for. I probably wouldn't have to spend my whole life in prison. After I got out, I might still be able to enjoy my dad's homemade bread and a game of Marco Polo in our above-ground pool.

Still, Grant lingered in my thoughts, and I worried whether he'd found a way out of the mess I'd created for him. Which reminded me—I'd promised to text Sophia. Maybe she would know what happened to Grant.

"Does someone have a phone I can use?" I asked, digging in my pocket for the piece of paper with Sophia's number on it.

Damien handed me his, and while my family celebrated around me, I texted Sophia: "I'm home now. Have you heard from Grant?" I figured she could read between the lines and recognize it was me.

I handed it back to Damien when I was done, but he shook his head. "You keep it." What a sacrifice. His phone had been attached to him like an extra appendage for the last nine months since he'd earned enough at his part-time job to afford it.

"Thank you, Damien." I could barely get the words out.

My family bombarded me with questions after that. I had to tell them all the details—or at least most of them—and Mom let everyone, even my ten-year-old sister stay up to hear everything. I left out a lot about Grant, especially the flirting, but I did tell them plenty about Sophia, Mr. Tilney, Clayton, and the guy from the trailer. There was so much to tell, and after about an hour, I'd reached my limit. "I'm really tired, guys. Do you mind if I finish explaining everything in the morning?"

"Sure," Dad said, kissing me on the forehead. "Mom's prayer group is coming over in the morning, so I think it's best if Eva and I stay the night out here in the playroom. We need a little more time to talk things through before she turns herself into the police. The rest of y'all can go ahead inside."

That sounded good to me. I hugged each one of them again, and then I laid down to sleep as my Dad sat outside the playroom door. Before I hit the pillow, though, I checked Damien's phone for a response from Sophia. Nothing had come through yet. I'd have to wait until the morning to find out if Grant had survived my betrayal.

CHAPTER 20

The first thing I did the next morning was check the phone, but that was a disappointment. I still didn't have a response from Sophia. Did that mean the whole Tilney family was in trouble? Or had my text not gone through?

I sent another text. "I got home fine. How are you? Please respond."

When I looked out the playhouse window, Dad was standing there with breakfast. He must have heard me stirring and gone to get food. It was good food too—Mom's special strawberry waffles with whipped butter.

Mom came out after her prayer group left. She sat on the mattress beside me. "Dad and I were talking about it, and we've decided we just want you to take some time to relax. If you want to sneak inside the house to take a shower, I don't think anyone's going to notice. While you're there, Dad's going to set up the extension cord, so you can catch up on all your computer things."

It did feel great to have a shower. On the other hand, being back on the computer didn't feel quite so wonderful. I was still too worried about Grant, and, remembering the videos Sophia showed me, I didn't have the heart to check my vlogs. Instead, I checked Damien's phone every few minutes, only to find that Sophia hadn't responded.

I was glad that Dad came in and played a few video games with me while the kids were at school. Then Mom came in just to talk.

I made sure I had a good view out the playhouse door, in case Mrs. Garland and her gang came around. I hadn't told my parents about meeting them at Granny Annie's. They'd worried enough. But I was sure Mrs. Garland was smart enough to know where I lived.

"Mom and I found a good lawyer we think can help you with your case," Dad said. He'd brought a chair inside the playhouse, and was pretending to read the newspaper. "We can pay for it."

"Okay," I said. "Thank you." It was probably time I called the police.

No, I'd wait for a couple more hours. I couldn't call the police until I heard back from Sophia. She should know about Grant by now—unless he'd had to go into hiding because of my mistake. Or unless something worse had happened. I tried not to think about that.

Later on, when my brothers and sisters got home from school, we played a few rounds of video games together. Then Dad brought us some pizza he had made for dinner. We sat in a circle on the floor of the playroom, eating pizza and laughing about silly things like the time Wade wore roller skates to prom and somehow got his date's hair caught in the wheels. Then they caught me up on all the things that had been going on since I'd left. Damien had gotten into more than one fight, defending my reputation, and he had the bruises to show for it.

"I'm sorry," I told him.

He grinned. "It was nothing. I don't mind getting suspended if I have to."

In the corner, Dad rolled his eyes. "There'll be no more fighting. Eva's back now. She can defend her own honor."

After the kids left to do homework, I went back online. Instead of checking my vlogs, I looked up the news. There didn't seem to be anything about my case or about Grant. Then, since I was going to turn myself in to the police the next day anyway, I did what Grant had told me to never do—I checked my e-mail. The only thing that wasn't spam in my inbox was a quick note from Beau, who used to be my best dating prospect. That was before I met Grant—the man who seemed to know me before he even knew my name. It was like Grant had read my whole personality just from looking at me that first afternoon at the diner. Beau was good-looking like Grant, but reading through his quick e-mail, in which he joked about how I might have disappeared because I'd been hungover from all my partying during spring break, I decided Beau didn't know me at all. At least not like Grant did.

But between our fight over the phone and what happened at Granny Annie's, I'd burned my bridges with Grant. It was time for a fresh start. I was going to become a forensic scientist. Maybe by the time I got my degree, the police wouldn't mind if I was an ex-felon. It'd give me an edge.

Did they let people study for degrees in prison?

Mom interrupted my thoughts. "Knock, knock," she called from outside the playhouse.

"Come in," I called back.

She stepped into the doorway, a deadpan expression on her face. "You have a visitor at the house." She paused at the word visitor, as if she suspected this might not be the kind of visitor I wanted to receive.

My heart thumped. Could it be that Grant had come to visit me? That would probably mean he'd forgiven me, and that things weren't as dire for him as I'd feared. Or perhaps it was Ronald or the guy from the trailer. "What did he look like?"

"She's an attractive young woman. She says you and she are working on an assignment together. She looks normal enough, but—"

An assignment. That could be any number of people from school, but why would they come by the house? They didn't even know my address. The only other young woman I could think of was Sophia, but her father would have never let her leave the house. Had Mrs. Garland sent someone to take care of me, someone I'd never seen before? "What did she look like?"

"Long, wavy hair."

It sounded like Sophia, but I wasn't taking any chances. I called the home phone and asked to speak to my visitor. I recognized Sophia's voice as soon as she said hello.

I exhaled in relief. "My mom said you needed help with an assignment."

"Desperately."

CHAPTER 21

In the peach orchard, pink petals littered the ground like confetti, and tiny green fruits were bursting forth where the blossoms had been. Sophia was already waiting there, sitting on an overturned bucket. She stood when she saw me coming and before I was even close enough to hand back her credit card, she called to me. "Grant sent me to apologize for him."

Grant was still alive. Relief flooded through me, and I let my body relax for the first time since I'd seen him at the truck stop. If he wanted to apologize, that meant he wasn't angry with me either. "You don't know how relieved I am to hear that."

"It's his fault you got into this mess," Sophia continued, "and my father's very sorry about the misunderstanding with Clayton."

"You didn't have to come all this way to tell me that."

"Grant made me promise it'd be the first thing I said."

She held two envelopes in her hand and handed me one of them. "He wanted me to give you this."

The words *For Eva* were scrawled on the front. I slid my finger under the seal, tore it open, and pulled out a letter.

"Go ahead and read it," Sophia said.

Dear Eva,

After all that has happened, I have no right to even contact you. It's my fault that you came into danger, and though I tried to protect you, I've only brought you into more danger than ever. I wouldn't blame you if you never forgave me.

I will always remember the days we spent together. As dangerous as it all was, I've never enjoyed myself more, and it was all because of you. You bring out the me in me more than any other person I know. Funny how it all started at that little diner and only lasted a little over 48 hours. I'm still looking forward to dessert. But unfortunately, because of current circumstances, that's looking less and less likely. Please know that my affection for you is real. It wasn't something I pretended as part of my job.

I held the letter to my chest. It was a real love letter, and every word added to my joy. He didn't think any of this was my fault, and he still cared about me. I wished I could talk to Grant right then and let him know that I returned his feelings. "Where is he?" I asked Sophia.

Sophia plucked a blade of grass and ran it through her fingers. "He managed to get out of Granny Annie's, thanks to your quick planning."

"So the truck drivers helped him?" I couldn't keep the excitement from my voice. Yes, Grant had been in peril, but I, Eva Morland, had played a part in rescuing him.

"Yes," she said. "Ronald pulled a knife on him in the parking lot, but the truckers took him down. Grant got home safe and sound—complete with a three-truck escort." Then she winced. "But he was so determined to finish what he started that he's gone back one last time. There's more on the back of that letter."

He wasn't safe, then? I turned back to the letter.

I'm afraid it may be a very long time before I will be able to see you again. It is safer for you if you don't try to find me. I have talked with the government agents, and they assure me that your case is clear. More importantly, I've made a bargain with our enemies, and I believe that they will leave you in peace from now on.

Please, for your own sake, don't try to contact me.
Love,
Grant

I turned to Sophia, everything in me rebelling against his last words. "I don't care if it's dangerous. I have to see him again."

"First," Sophia said, "I think you'd better sit down. I need to tell you some things."

I overturned two buckets, sat on one, and motioned for her to sit down on the other "I've been on the run for the last week. Whatever you have to say can't make me any more worried."

She sat down across from me, but her gaze wandered to the other side of the orchard. "I had a talk with my dad yesterday after

147

you left. I demanded to see pictures of my mother and to be allowed to contact her." She kept her voice low, as if she were ashamed of herself.

"Good for you," I said, expecting it must have been difficult for her to confront her father that way.

"It finally all makes sense to me—why they split up, why mom would leave me, why I wouldn't be able to contact her ever."

"Really?" I couldn't see how losing her mother could ever make sense.

"Yes. My dad threw her out all those years ago because she was involved in the exotic animal trade."

My mouth hung open. That wasn't what I was expecting to hear at all. I wasn't sure I even knew what it was. "Exotic animal trade?"

"She ships monkeys and other jungle animals from Mexico and South America to people here in America and Canada. Some people use them for pets, but others use them for food or for their skins. She started getting into the business when I was a little girl. Dad never approved of it. That's why they split up. The longer Mom was involved in it, the more Dad saw how cruel it was. So many of the animals died in transport, and their owners were sometimes neglectful."

That meant her father was the good parent of the two. I hadn't expected that. "So all those trophy animals in the garage belonged to—"

Sophia finished my sentence for me. "My mom. She wouldn't give up the business—she liked the money too much—but she agreed with my father that it was important to protect us children. So they made an agreement that my father would have full custody of us. My mother would change her name and give up her role as our mother. She promised she wouldn't try to contact me or Grant."

Poor Sophia and Grant! How must they feel, knowing their mother would choose a life of crime over them? "I'm so sorry. That's horrible."

"Mom kept her promise not to ever contact me, but when Grant went to college, she sent him gifts, took him out to dinner, even took him on a tour of Europe—all while swearing Grant to secrecy. Because of her success in trafficking, she had much more money than Dad could ever have. After a while, Grant told Dad that he'd been spending time with Mom, and Dad was furious, which caused a rift between him and Grant for a time."

I kicked a little at the grass below my feet. I'd been all wrong about Mr. Tilney. "Now I can see why your dad tries so hard to protect you."

"Yeah. If you're going to blame one of my parents, blame my mom. That's what I do now." She gave me the saddest look, but her words had a hard edge to them. "My mother abandoned me."

I could see why Mr. Tilney wanted Sophia to take all her college courses online. He didn't want her anywhere near her mother's influence. "Why didn't he tell you all this before?"

"I think he didn't want me to know my mother was a criminal, especially when I was younger."

I nodded. If Sophia had known her mom was a criminal, she might have questioned whether she could grow up to be the same way.

She handed me the other envelope. "I think you might recognize my mom."

A chill ran through me. "Your mom isn't—" I opened the envelope and flipped through the photos inside. Yes, she was younger and softer, holding a little Sophia on her lap, but the face was unmistakable. It was Mrs. Garland. "She's the one who kidnapped me."

Sophia nodded, gazing down at her hands. The shame her father had wanted to prevent was already evident. "My mother's name is Candace Tilney, but since she left us, she's used a few different aliases. Federal agents promised Grant that if he can convince Mom to provide them with a list of buyers and suppliers, it will save her from years in prison. That's why Grant quit his job and asked Mom to let him work with her. He helps run the cover business, which is contract shipping. He never handles illegal shipments."

"That sounds like Grant," I said.

149

"He didn't tell Mom that his real goal is to find proof of her illegal shipments. Once he gets enough proof, he'll tell her that if she doesn't turn herself in, he will. But I'm afraid he's gotten in too deep. It's not just Mom he needs to worry about. It's the people she works with that are the real danger. They'll do anything to keep from being discovered."

I shivered. After the last week, I understood the fear of going to prison. The people who worked with Grant's mom were probably willing to commit any crime if it meant they'd stay free. They certainly wouldn't have a problem killing Grant to avoid a lifetime behind bars. "And now I've made things even worse for him," I said.

"Grant said they still think you're Leslie Kaplan—"

"—and that I'm a government spy." But now that they'd seen us together, they would know Grant was working with the government too. Why else would Leslie Kaplan know him so well?

We had to convince them somehow that Grant and I weren't working together. Sophia had been right to make me sit down. Things were worse than I'd thought. "I'll do anything to help him. Just tell me what to do."

"The only thing Dad and I can think of that would help solve the problem is if you could let Grant kill you." She didn't seem to be joking.

The breeze died down. Had she really said that?

She tilted her head to the side and closed one eye. "Not really kill you. Pretend to kill you. If my mother and her gang saw that Grant was willing to shoot someone he cares about for their cause, they might trust him again." She bent toward me. "Dad and I figured out a way to do it without you getting hurt."

I leaned back. "Does Grant know about this?"

"He would never ask that kind of thing of you. But it's the only solution we can see. Grant's up at Mom's house in Montana right now. We'll have to go up there."

The wind blew through the orchard, shaking the last few blossoms from the trees. I'd have to leave my family again. They'd be worried. And I might have to face down Grant's mom and Ronald once again. This could get me in even more trouble than I

150

was already in. But if it meant saving Grant's life, I had no choice. "I'll do it."

Chapter 22

I'd promised myself that I wouldn't set foot inside my parents' house again until everything had cleared up, and now that everything was cleared up, my first priority was another shower. It was a quick one—Sophia wanted to leave as soon as possible.

Mom and Dad were waiting for me when I came out of the bathroom, wearing my bathrobe. "Hi, honey," Dad said. They'd never been hover parents before my kidnapping. I'd broken them.

"Hi ... um." I couldn't stand to leave them again. If it hadn't been for Grant, I wouldn't have. "I wanted to let you know I'll be heading north tonight. I'll probably be back in a few days."

The fact that I was leaving so soon made my mom and dad send questioning looks between them.

"I promise I'll keep in touch better this time," I said. "I'll use Sophia's phone."

"Are you sure it wouldn't be better to talk to a lawyer?" Mom asked, clasping her hands as if in prayer. "I can make an appointment for you. I think that would be a much safer thing for you."

It about killed me to tell her no after all the worry I'd caused her. "Sorry, mom, this is something I have to do to help my friend, Grant. I'll be as careful as I can."

I walked to my bedroom to grab some warm clothes Sophia told me I'd need for our trip. As I grabbed a coat from my closet, mom stood in the doorway, her lips pressed together and her arms folded tight across her chest.

"We trust you," Mom said, her voice gruff. "You know that. We don't believe anything we've heard on the news about you. But we do worry about your safety. Are you sure this is a smart idea right now?"

I cleared my throat. It wasn't a smart or a safe idea. It was the only idea. How could I explain that? "I'm not worried about myself anymore. Grant told me the police have dropped the charges against me. But now he's in trouble, and if I don't go, I'll regret it for the rest of my life." With that, I hugged my parents. "I love you," I said. "I'll be back as soon as I can."

They watched me as if they were frozen with their arms crossed, bracing for another week of worry.

The image of my parents stayed in my brain as Sophia and I drove away from the farm. I was expecting to be in the car for hours, but after only one hour, Sophia turned into a little airport outside Houston. It was around eight p.m. "What are we doing here?" I asked.

"Meeting Dad."

Though I was feeling better about her dad, I still hadn't gotten over the fact that he had thought I was a liar. Now I was going to have to talk to him again. Would he apologize, or would he pretend nothing had happened? "We're driving with your dad?"

"We're flying with my dad. He has his own plane."

I remembered Sophia saying something about him having to travel a lot for work and how he had his own plane because of it. I just never thought I'd have to fly with him. I'd flown before, but I'd only traveled on major commercial airlines. Whatever little airplane Mr. Tilney flew wouldn't be nearly as stable, and it's not like there'd be a copilot if anything happened to Mr. Tilney. I wiped my palms on my pants.

We parked in a gravel lot and walked out to the hangar, where Mr. Tilney was waiting. He looked the same as ever in a pair of gray slacks and a button-up shirt with his gray hair combed to the side. "Hello, Eva," he said, as if he hadn't ever planned to call the police on me and I hadn't just agreed to risk my life for his son. As if I was the one who'd caused this whole problem. And he did have a point, but this problem didn't begin with me. If I hadn't met Grant in that diner, my life would be a lot simpler right now. I would've been off somewhere studying calculus with Beau, blissfully unaware of any dangerous and thrilling adventure I could have had with a much better man.

"Hello, Mr. Tilney," I said. If he wasn't going to apologize, I wasn't either.

He took my bag and then looked me up and down. "This plane has a weight limit. I'm going to need your weight, and I need you to be honest about it." He passed me his phone and motioned for me to enter the number into the calculator. "Pounds, not kilograms."

As if I would put kilograms. I almost typed in 250, just to see what he would say, but then I remembered that this was about saving Grant, so I put in 132, which was a whole five pounds more than I'd put on my driver's license.

I handed him back the calculator. "By the way, what happened to Slurpee after I left?"

"He's staying with a neighbor that lives about a mile from us," Sophia said. "She'll take good care of him until we get back. She loves animals."

Mr. Tilney pressed a few keys on the calculator. Then he looked me up and down again. "Okay. Let's get going."

The plane was a white Cessna. I'd seen plenty of them flying above our farm. Around where we lived, farmers mostly used little planes like that for crop dusting.

Being inside one was a different story, however. It was quite obvious that this plane had been built before my birth. There was nothing digital about it. Everything on the dashboard was a dial, and the upholstery was a mix of tan plaid and vinyl. Sure, I usually loved anything vintage, but not vintage technology. When it came to planes, I was all for digital displays and LED lights. As Mr. Tilney put on his headset and radioed the flight tower, I put on my retrofitted gray seatbelt. Before he headed for the runway, he turned around in his seat and asked, "Have you ever taken an acting class, Eva?"

"I took drama in high school." Back then, I was only in it for the costumes. I didn't know I would have to fake my own death one day.

"Did you learn anything about stage fighting?"

"No, sir."

"Well," he said with a shrug. "You'll just have to do your best. You can start studying the plans while we're in the air." He handed me a file folder full of papers and a pen light. Flipping through, I saw instructions about how to open a locked door with a credit card and something that looked like the floorplans for a house. "You'll also need these," he said, handing me a couple of earplugs. "It gets pretty loud in here."

Soon we were racing down the runway, my heart pounding against my chest. I looked out the tiny window as we lifted off the ground, hoping to catch sight of a familiar landmark. It was growing dark and the lights below sparkled like thousands of rhinestones. Soon, though, as we left the city behind, the pattern of lights grew sparser.

Turning my attention away from the window, I clicked on the penlight and read through the folder Mr. Tilney had given me. I had to wonder if Mr. Tilney really expected me to open locked doors or find my way around the home that was detailed in the drawings. Did I really need to know about someone else's security systems and passcodes? Was I actually going to deal with guard dogs? It seemed way too illegal, and I had to keep reminding myself that I was doing this to save Grant. I was one of the good guys.

The information in the folder was so detailed that I couldn't help closing my eyes to rest. Maybe if I took a catnap, I could concentrate better. "How long is this flight going to be?" I yelled to Sophia, who was sitting by her father at the front of the plane.

"Five hours," she yelled back.

Plenty of time for a nap. I put my coat over me for a blanket and closed my eyes. It'd just be for a few minutes. Then I'd get back to studying the folder.

The next thing I knew, it was dark and we were coming down for a landing. It was also freezing cold for springtime. I pulled my coat on and zipped it up. Popping out my ear plugs and leaning forward, I yelled, "Where are we?"

Sophia turned to me. "We're taking a pit stop in Denver. Then we'll head up near Yellowstone."

The clock read 12:30. I pointed to it. "Is that really the time?" I asked.

Sophia nodded. "Dad always changes the clock to local time."

155

I found a blanket on the seat next to me and wrapped myself up in it. There was white stuff on the ground below us. "Is that snow?" I yelled.

Mr. Tilney answered this time. "An early spring snow. There'll be even more of it in Montana."

We didn't get much snow in Texas. The largest snowman I'd ever built had been about two feet tall. So, after we got off the plane, I found the nearest patch of snow and started on what I hoped to be my largest snowman ever. The snow glowed bright in the airport lights, so it wasn't hard to see, despite it being after midnight.

Once Mr. Tilney had fueled up the plane, he and Sophia walked over and watched as I rolled snow into a ball for the middle of my snowman. This one was going to be at least three feet tall— a definite record for me. After a minute, he tilted his head back and laughed. I sat up, wondering what I'd done wrong this time. Mr. Tilney was laughing?

He shook his head. "I don't know how I could have ever believed that college kid who said you came from a rich family."

Sophia picked up a ball of snow and threw it at him, hitting him in the chest. "You should have listened to Grant. He told you Eva was just a normal girl from the country."

He dusted off his jacket. "It wouldn't have been the first time Grant was wrong about a woman. But I guess this time, I was the one in the wrong."

I smiled. It was the first nice thing he'd said about me. "Thank you, Mr. Tilney."

He helped me roll a ball of snow for the head and then held the middle steady while I placed the head on top. "Come on," he said. "Let's get something to eat before we go back on the plane … and before you freeze to death."

Several small airlines operated from this airport, so we made our way toward one of their hubs. Inside, we found some tables and chairs near a few vending machines. Mr. Tilney treated us to hot cocoa and a bag of trail mix. I couldn't have been happier if he'd taken me to a five-star restaurant. I finally had his approval.

Yes, I was about to risk my life for his son, so I totally deserved his approval. But it had been a long time coming.

"Have you ever been to Yellowstone?" he asked as we sat down together.

"No." Having visited only a few National Parks, they all blended together in my mind—Yellowstone and Yosemite might as well have been the same place.

"We might get to see some grizzly bears and bison," Sophia explained.

That's when a distant memory dawned on me—from my parents' honeymoon scrapbook. Hadn't they gone to Yellowstone? I remembered a picture of them kissing in front of an enormous geyser. "And Old Faithful?"

"We might get to see that too if there's time."

I pictured Grant kissing me in front of Old Faithful, just like in my parents' old pictures. Maybe this was going to be fun—after the part where I broke into someone's house and pretended to die.

Mr. Tilney excused himself, and Sophia leaned closer to me. "I don't know if I want to see my mom," she whispered.

"You don't have to see her," I said. I wouldn't have set foot anywhere near Grant's mom if I didn't have to, and it wasn't like she deserved a visit after abandoning her only daughter, but I kept my opinion to myself. I wasn't going to make Sophia feel any worse about her mom than she already did.

"I want to see what she's like. I have this image of her in my mind, sitting on the sofa, painting her nails in her fluffy pink bathrobe. She used to paint my nails too, and we'd go shopping for clothes at nice stores. I used to love shopping with her." She stirred the hot cocoa in her cup and frowned. "I've hated shopping ever since she left."

"I'll bet she hates shopping now too," I said, and remembering the rodeo get-up her mother had on when she kidnapped me, I halfway believed that she really did hate shopping. She could have easily gotten that thing fifteen years earlier.

Sophia glanced down the hallway. "Dad doesn't want me to see her," she whispered.

"I can see his point." Now that I could see the whole picture, it was easier to understand why Mr. Tilney was so strict a father. All the advice I'd heard in the past about avoiding toxic people was coming back to me. It could be harmful for Sophia to renew her relationship with her mother.

"I can see his point too," Sophia said. "As I child, I used to make up stories about her that made her seem better than she really is. I feel like it's time I faced the truth."

A door opened, and Mr. Tilney emerged from the men's restroom.

I leaned toward Sophia and squeezed her hand. "Whatever you decide to do, I'll support you."

Sophia flashed me a quick smile before she turned her attention to her dad.

"We'd better get going. We're scheduled to depart in a few minutes," he said. It was now past one a.m.

We boarded the plane and took off, heading for Montana. The stars twinkled above us while the lights from Denver twinkled below. I didn't go to sleep at all on this flight, thinking about everything that I was going to have to do when I got there. I flipped through the pages in the folder that Mr. Tilney had given me, studying the layouts and trying to memorize methods for breaking into homes. If I didn't feel so bad about getting Grant into this mess and knowing I was his best option of getting out, I would have never agreed to come at all. I wasn't the type to break and enter. And yet … the idea of opening locked doors and windows fascinated me.

Buried in the mess of papers was a handwritten skit of sorts, showing how I was supposed to play out my death. "Please Memorize!" Mr. Tilney had written at the top. Surely, he didn't expect me to deliver a canned speech. There had to be some adlibbing involved. Still, I did my best to memorize the gist of the dialogue.

We landed at another small airport around two a.m. Snow was still on the ground, and I'm not talking a dusting of snow like there was in Denver. A foot of snow covered everything except the roads. Mr. Tilney called for a ride to a rental car company, where we chose a four-wheel-drive Jeep. We drove through the blinding snow on small roads and then on smaller roads until we came to West Yellowstone, a little tourist town, where the prevalent decorating theme seemed to be log. I'd never been to a place where log cabins had gingerbread trim. It was quaint and cute. I would have loved to stay here for fun. Why couldn't I just be a tourist instead of an undercover actor? It wasn't to be, though. Tonight, I checked into my room under the name of Leslie Kaplan.

"I'll find another place to stay," Mr. Tilney said, handing Sophia the car keys. "I think it's best if we aren't seen together, but call me if you need anything. I'll stay close."

After he walked off, I got out the folder and flipped through it again, mouthing the words to my script a few times over.

"I don't think I'll be able to sleep at all," I told Sophia. The reality of what I had agreed to do was sinking in.

She flipped the light switch off, making the room only slightly dimmer, thanks to the porch light outside our window. "Everything depends on you, Eva. You need to take care of yourself."

That didn't make me feel any less anxious. After Sophia fell asleep, I snuck into the bathroom and watched videos about how to open locks with credit cards. Whoever said video blogs weren't useful? Yes, the same video could have been used by a real criminal, but, from the comments, I guessed that most of the people who used the technique had simply locked themselves out of the house. Maybe I could do this after all. It didn't look that hard.

I went back to bed and somehow, after rehearsing that death script in my head a few times, I was so exhausted, I fell asleep despite all my worries.

Sophia woke me at a quarter to nine the next morning. "I'm sorry, Eva, but the continental breakfast is about to end. Do you want anything?"

Did I have to remind her that I came from a family of ten children? I was out of bed and getting dressed within seconds. "I hope they have one of those flip-over waffle irons."

They didn't.

But they did have a variety of individually wrapped pastries that my mother would have frowned upon. I gulped down a cherry strudel and toasted myself a chocolate Pop Tart. Sophia crinkled her nose as she watched me, but the way I saw it, this could have been my last breakfast ever. I might as well indulge.

"Dad brought over a winter coat and boots for you this morning." She leaned toward me, whispering. "You're supposed to squeeze the right breast of the coat after Grant shoots you. There's a blood packet in there that will make it look like you're bleeding."

My dread must have shown on my face because she quickly added, "I'm sure you'll do great."

Back in our room, she showed me the white down coat with a faux fur rim around the hood. I slipped into it, careful not to squeeze it anywhere, and then put on the shoes. "Let's do this," I said, sticking my hands in the pockets to find a pair of gloves, Leslie Kaplan's credit card, and some tools to open locks.

Sophia opened her eyes wide. "Are you sure?"

"Yes." Ready or not, I was going to Grant's mom's house.

We drove out into the wilderness with snow flying around the Jeep. All around us, tall evergreens rose to the sky. "It's a good thing it's snowing," Sophia said, a fake smile on her face. "That'll help you hide better."

Even with my new coat and boots, I shivered. I didn't know how to walk through deep snow, much less act out my own death. But, at least, Grant would be expecting me. I had to keep marching forward for him.

Sophia's navigation app stopped us at the end of a long driveway that had been plowed enough to show patches of asphalt under the snow and ice. "This is it," Sophia said. "The house is at the end of the drive. Grant's inside. He knows the plan." She took a small handgun from the glove compartment and handed it to me. "It's loaded with blanks."

Somehow, I put the gun in my pocket, got out of the car, and waved to Sophia as she drove off. I started up the driveway, noticing how someone had spread salt on the icy patches. Had Grant done that? Or were there other people living and working there? When I'd read through the script, I'd pictured just Grant and his mother being home. What if there were others too—like Ronald and the guy from the trailer? Had Mr. Tilney bothered to check? Surely, he would have communicated with Grant about this. Sophia wouldn't have brought me here if it didn't look like I could succeed.

Trudging up the hill, my feet slipped on an icy patch, and I fell, catching myself with my hands. I got back up, dusting the snow off my knees, the way I'd seen people do on movies. I checked the coat, making sure I hadn't pierced the blood packet. Luckily, it was still intact.

Snow fell around me, and it struck me that under any other circumstances, I would love this. I was literally walking in a winter wonderland. It was probably one of the most beautiful places on earth. "Come on, Eva," I said out loud, "just pretend this is a vacation."

It still didn't feel like vacation, but saying it gave me the courage I needed to keep trudging up the hill. At least I was going to see Grant. A few days ago, I'd given up hope of even that.

I came around a bend in the driveway, and the house appeared in front of me behind a trimmed hedge of boxwood bushes. I'd expected something tall and stately, perhaps with natural stone walls or brick. What faced me was an oversized Mediterranean Villa with arched windows and stucco walls as white as the snow around it. Somehow the house plans hadn't been enough to help me picture this.

I stepped off the driveway, wading through the snow until I got to the back of the house. There was no fence, making it easy to find the back deck I'd learned about in the diagrams. Creeping up to the foundation of the house and turning a corner past the back deck, I found some cement stairs leading to the basement. There was the door I was supposed to unlock—a plain, white, metal door. I slid the credit card down the way I'd learned. It went past the deadbolt—Grant had left that open as planned. But the card caught on the latch beside the doorknob. I pushed down, but it wouldn't budge. This was going to be harder than I thought. I tried again, this time trying to turn the knob with my other hand. My hands were already aching from cold. From inside the house, I could hear chirping and squeaking. The animals must have been close by, and they were crying out a warning to the rest of the house. I'd have to act fast.

I gritted my teeth. This had to work. It simply had to. Grant was depending on me. I knew he wouldn't let me down if I were the one who needed rescuing.

I uttered a prayer under my breath. I was doing this for a good cause, after all. This wasn't the average break-in. I was doing this to save a life, and I needed all the help I could get. "Please, God, make this work."

I took a deep breath to calm myself and then slid the card down as hard as I could, keeping it flat to the side of the doorframe. Voilá. I turned the knob and pulled the door open as the animals inside sent up their jungle alarms. Then I caught my breath as their stink wafted toward me—something between old cat pee and dead skunk.

I could do this. At least, the air was warm. Holding my nose, I peeked inside the large, unfinished basement to see rows of metal dog crates with animals of all sorts inside. There were black, gold, and gray monkeys, some as small as my hand. Along the back wall, blue parrots squawked in their cages. And right beside me, in the largest cage of all, hissed a leopard. Quickly closing the door behind me, I darted to the other side of the room—that leopard cage didn't look strong enough to me.

I stood still, between a space heater and the only door leading out of the room, aching for the little creatures who'd been kidnapped from their jungle homes, only to end up caged in an unfinished basement. I didn't have time to help them now, though. I had to find the stairs leading upstairs. That's where I was supposed to meet Grant.

I opened the next door and crept into another large room, this one stacked wall to wall with shelves of plastic boxes and aquariums. Inside, hundreds of reptiles languished—baby crocodilians, lizards, snakes, and turtles of all sorts. What little I knew about reptiles came from my brother Wade, who'd often brought snakes and lizards home from his adventures on our farms, and these containers didn't look nearly as large as the ones Wade had used. In this room, which had been framed and covered with unpainted drywall, I found two doors. When I approached the first door, something on the other side growled. Opening the door a crack, I caught sight of a white wolf in a large crate. At least, I thought it was a wolf. Whatever it was, it was baring its teeth in a way my dogs at home never would. I shut the door, hoping I wouldn't have to go inside that room.

Luckily, behind the other door, I found a carpeted staircase, leading upstairs, where I would find Grant—and whoever else might be waiting. Surely, they'd heard all the commotion already. The staircase was dark, but I didn't dare switch on a light. Instead, I closed the door behind me, blocking all the light from the reptile room. That way, if someone did open the upstairs door, I'd be able to see them better than they saw me.

I took the stairs one at a time, straining to hear any noises from upstairs. It seemed as if no one was home at all. Grant wouldn't do that to me, though. He would make sure everything was in place. He would know how hard it would be for me to confront the same people who'd kidnapped me. He wouldn't let me fail.

At the top of the staircase, I twisted the knob and cracked the door open. Peeking out, I saw a large oil painting of flowers, white carpet, and nothing else. I had to do this, and I had to do it fast. The longer I waited, the more likely it was that something would go wrong.

"Five, four, three, two, one," I counted in my head. Then I pushed open the door and stepped out. I was in the entryway of an expansive house—the kind I'd seen in movies with a grand staircase and a tall ceiling that went all the way to the second floor. I crept across the soft carpet.

A scream filled the air, and I jumped, my gaze darting toward the sound. It was a red macaw. He was climbing the walls of an enormous black cage. "Not again," he squawked. "Visitors."

I heard a door open above and looked up to see Mrs. Garland emerge, staring down at me from behind the banister. It was hard to think of her as Grant's mother, Candace Tilney. Their personalities weren't at all alike, even if their features matched.

Her hair was different this time. She'd cut it short and added red highlights. She was wearing a dark green dressing gown with a fur trim. If I hadn't despised her so much, I would have admired her fashion sense. That trim was probably real fur too, which made me despise her all the more.

She chuckled. "Leslie?"

Where was Grant?

It didn't matter. This was my cue. I had to speak. "I've figured out your plan," I said, sinking my voice to its deepest pitch, "and I want in on it."

I pointed the gun at her, just like we'd planned. Grant was supposed to have taken her gun away somehow, so I'd be safe. "I want in on your business. Otherwise, I'm turning you in."

Candace threw her head back and laughed, looking like she was having the time of her life. "Oh, is that right?"

It was then that Grant came into the room, pulling his own gun on me. "I heard the bird. What's going on?" Then he turned his back to his mother and approached me with the gun. "Leslie, you don't want to do this. Put the gun down."

"I do want to do this. You've ruined my life, Grant."

"Put the gun down or I'll shoot."

Aiming well to the left of Grant's head, even though it was a blank, I squeezed the trigger. Bang. The gun kicked in my hands. Grant didn't move, just continued to aim at my chest with his back to his mother. He mouthed the words one, two, three. Then he shot me with his blank, and I fell into a heap on the floor. I gripped the little packet in my breast pocket until I could feel the liquid flowing out. My hair had fallen across my face, just as I'd planned, so that Candace wouldn't be able to see whether I was breathing.

I heard footsteps approaching. "What was that noise?" The voice drove all the warmth from my limbs. It was the same voice I'd heard in the warehouse on the day I was kidnapped. Ronald's voice.

"It was nothing," Candace said, her tone dull. "Grant just took care of some business for me."

Grant fell to his knees beside me, bending over me and placing his finger on my neck, pretending to feel for a pulse.

"Grant took care of—is that the girl that," Ronald began.

"You'd better leave, Ronald," Candace said, "in case one of the neighbors heard and sent for the police."

"So it's time for the escape plan?" Ronald's voice was quieter this time.

"Exactly. Where's Paulo?"

Who was Paulo? Was he the man from the trailer?

"He's in the garage," Ronald answered. "You told us you wanted us to prepare the truck to make a shipment."

"Oh, yes, that's right. You'd better hurry and get him." The footsteps thumped past me, and another door opened

"You picked a bad place for that to happen," Candace said from above. "I'm not sure we'll ever get the blood out of that carpet."

Grant didn't respond. Maybe he was too shocked that she would react that way, or maybe he was just pretending to be shocked. After about thirty more seconds, he said, "I'll clean it up. You don't have to worry about it."

"Well, you better do it fast," she said, "in case someone heard the shots."

"I'll do it fast" he said, a harsh edge to his words.

I heard footsteps from above and then the slam of a door. Did that mean Candace had left?

"Not Again," the macaw cried. "Not again."

Grant squeezed my hand, and I had the strongest urge to wrap my arms around him and kiss him, but I resisted, staying as still as possible. "Sorry about this," he whispered, taking hold of my other hand and pulling until I was on my back and he was dragging me across the carpet. "Stay limp," he whispered.

165

He was dragging me instead of picking me up? That wasn't what I'd expected. If he had been a real murderer, though, it's exactly what he would do. He wouldn't pick me up, as if I were his new bride. Nope, dragging was much more convincing.

Footsteps approached again, and Grant stopped, still holding my arms. I kept my head turned to the side, so my hair would cover my face.

"We have the computers and all the paperwork," Ronald said. He was closer this time, so I guessed he was speaking to Grant. "Are you coming to the airport with us?"

"No," he said. "I've got to clean up. You go ahead."

The footsteps rushed past us. Another door slammed. Then I heard the moan of a garage door opening.

Grant paused, waiting. His hands warmed mine. "You okay?" he whispered.

I gave the slightest nod.

I heard the garage door turn on again. Probably this time, it was closing. I hoped that meant Ronald and Paulo had left.

Grant placed my arms gently on the floor before opening a door and dragging me through it. There, the floor changed to a smoother surface. Allowing my eyelids to open slightly, I saw a washer and dryer. Grant let go of me again as he opened another door, leaving me to lie on my back. "Stairs," he muttered. Then, I felt his arms slipping below my shoulder and knees. Before I knew what was happening, he had cradled me in his arms and lifted me.

This wasn't exactly what I'd imagined when I'd fantasized about a man carrying me over a threshold—me playing dead with my arms and legs hanging limp as if I were being lugged around by Frankenstein. Not being able to wrap my arms around his neck was the worst kind of torture, and I was going to have to give him a stern lecture about it later on.

But I couldn't be upset. His touch calmed me, and my breathing slowed to match his. We were together again. How could anything be wrong? I'd thought I'd lost him, but here I was, back in his arms.

In the past, the thought of spending my life with one man had scared me, but now, I allowed the thought to linger.

166

After carrying me down the stairs into the garage, he paused. He'd left the lights off, but, opening my eyes a slit, I saw a black SUV in front of us. I could feel him shifting my weight to one side. "Uh uh," I muttered while keeping my mouth shut. I grew up with nine siblings. I knew what would happen if he tried to dig out his keys while still carrying me. No matter how buff he thought he was, he wasn't that strong.

He shifted my weight back again. "It's locked," he grumbled under his breath, "and the keys are in my pocket. Sorry."

Slowly, he crouched and laid me on the cold, cement floor. He did it as gently as if I were a sleeping baby going down for a nap—except for my head, which banged down onto the cement. I was a good enough actor to let that happen. "Sorry," he whispered. Keeping one hand on my arm, he pulled out his keys with the other. The car binged and he opened the hatch. Then he lifted me again, this time, placing me behind the back row of seats in the SUV.

Only, he didn't leave me there, like a normal criminal would. He sat beside me and pulled the door shut. "Are you okay?" he asked.

I didn't bother answering. I reached for him, pulling him toward me and delivering the kiss I'd been waiting to give him. I'd done all this for him, and I wanted him to know that. For a few seconds, the world around us disappeared. This was the real deal. He was the best man I'd ever known, the kind of man I could see spending the rest of my life with. Unlike most guys, he had guts. He had stepped into a crime ring to rescue his mother. But he was also sensitive and caring.

He smoothed the hair away from my face. "I have to tell you that when Dad asked me for plans of the house, I had no idea he was going to ask you to come do this. I would have never put you in so much danger. Until this morning, all I knew was that I needed to fill a gun with blanks and turn off the security system."

"You're welcome," I said, faking a frown.

"Thank you," he said, kissing my forehead. "You were absolutely amazing. I don't know how much longer Ronald could have held off from killing me."

I raised myself on my knees to kiss his forehead. "You're welcome again. I'm sorry about that whole thing at Granny Annie's. I should have never gone there. I feel like it's my fault Ronald wanted to kill you."

"None of this was your fault," he began, but he stopped, pulling me down to lie on the floor of the trunk. "The lights just came on," he whispered. "I think Mom's coming. Go back to playing dead."

I wanted to scream, but I couldn't have if I'd tried. My throat had closed off. She wasn't coming in the car, was she?

He threw a blanket over me and scrambled over the back seat into the front of the car.

One of the SUV's doors opened. "I'll tell you where to take the body," Mrs. Garland said.

"I already know what to do with it, Mom. You can stay home."

The seat squeaked as she sat down. "No, I'm coming with you."

A few seconds passed before Grant spoke again. "I think it's better for me to go alone. If someone sees—"

"—no one is going to see if you go where I want you to go." She sounded so calm about it, as if it had cost her nothing to watch me die. My anger returned and I almost wished I still had that gun Mr. Tilney gave me, and that it had something in it other than blanks. If only I had a cord or something to strangle her with—something like a belt. I was wearing a belt. If Grant didn't do something fast, I might leap across the back seat and choke her with it.

"Okay," Grant said, drawing out the word, "tell me where you want me to go." He was trying to play along with her, I guessed, but I wasn't waiting around to see what would happen. I unbuckled the belt I'd worn with my jeans.

"I have to show you where to go," she commanded. A car door slammed shut. "Start driving."

He still didn't start the car. Instead, he heaved a sigh. "Mom, I'd rather do this my way." His voice was beginning to take on an angry tone. I had to act fast. With my belt unbuckled, I inched it through the loops of my jeans.

"You really cared about that girl." She laughed. What was so funny about him caring about me? "Okay," she said, holding back another laugh. "Okay. Do it your way. Go ahead. Start driving already."

"I need to do this alone." His voice was so loud, my muscles tensed. I didn't dare move. "You obviously don't care about my feelings. Just get out of the car."

I waited to hear a door open. It didn't. Under the blanket, I wrapped the belt around one hand and then the other.

She was still laughing, but now she'd started clapping too. Why would she be clapping? "Great performance," she said. "You just got one thing wrong."

"Mom," Grant said, sounding even more irritated. "Can you stop being so dramatic. This is serious. I just shot a woman I cared about."

"You left her gun behind."

Stupid me! I'd dropped the gun when Grant pretended to shoot me. She'd probably checked and found it was loaded with blanks.

"I'm done asking you nicely," Grant said.

I pressed myself against the backseat, hoping she couldn't hear the sound of my breathing.

"Come on out, Leslie darling," Candace called. "You might as well join in the conversation."

This was probably a good time for me to jump out from behind the back seat and strangle her with my belt, but Grant spoke just as I threw off my blanket. "Why don't we let Eva go? She doesn't have anything to do with this."

Mrs. Garland laughed again. "I'm willing to bet my life that your gun has blanks too." He must have pointed his gun at her. He was willing to do that for me. "It's a good thing Ronald and Paulo didn't notice before they left for the airport."

"So you're not going to tell them?"

"Of course not. In fact, I think it's time we both bowed out. You're much better at being a lawyer, and it's about time I retired, don't you think?"

"Hallelujah," Grant said and turned on the ignition. "Let's take Eva back to a safe place. Then we'll talk about your retirement." The garage door began to open.

Her retirement? Did that mean she was going to turn herself in, or did that mean she was going to fly off to some South American country, where she would live out the rest of her days in luxury while I paid for her crimes?

Was this retirement idea another one of her tricks? From what I knew about her, she had no intention of ever owning up to her sins, nor would she mind hurting me again. She might not even mind hurting Grant.

If I hadn't still been inside Candace's garage, I would have jumped straight out of that car and made a run for it. I decided, though, it'd be better to wait until we were closer to civilization.

As Grant drove out of the garage, Candace spoke again. "I'm afraid I must apologize about the way I've managed this whole affair. You see, I always suspected there was something going on between you and that Leslie Kaplan. I told Ronald I wanted him to bring Leslie to me if they could ever find her. Of course, they never could find her—she wasn't a real person, was she?"

"No," Grant said. "She wasn't."

"A very clever trick you played on us. But then Eva came along, saying she was Leslie, and Ronald bungled the whole thing. I had to save face, so I set off those bug bombs. I made sure to open the door after we set off a few of them, so that no one's life would be threatened. I'm sorry if I scared you, Eva." She spoke as if I were a kindergartener.

I was too shocked to respond. She made it all sound so innocent, but it hadn't been at all. The reek of those bug bombs was still fresh in my mind. She'd tried to kill me in that awful trailer home, and as for the door, I was the one who left it open so that Ronald and Ingrid wouldn't die.

She went on talking to me. "When and Paulo found out you'd gone to the police, Eva, they decided to frame you. They had the janitor give Clayton that address—the house belongs to a friend of mine, who happened to owe me quite a bit of money. Anyway, they set up the whole thing—the scream, the terracotta figurine, the security camera. And just like we expected, you went to the rescue when Ingrid screamed."

"By the way" Grant said. "Eva should know that Ingrid wasn't injured at all. She faked the whole thing."

Candace chuckled—or was it more of a cackle? "I really am sorry about the armed robbery allegations."

"Are you really?" Anger overtook me as I remembered how the video made it look like I'd attacked Ingrid to get her purse. I couldn't stay quiet anymore. "If you're so sorry about all of it," I said, popping my head up from behind the backseat, "why don't you turn yourself in? That way, my reputation might not be ruined forever. You've already done extensive damage to my vlogging career. I'm not sure my fan base—what few of them there are—will ever recover from this."

Candace turned to face me, her lips pursed. "Have you seen the number of people watching your little vlogs? It's quadrupled since your kidnapping. I've done you a favor, Leslie—or Eva."

My vlog traffic had quadrupled? This whole time I'd thought—wait, she hadn't said anything about turning herself into the police.

Grant stopped the car as we came to the end of the long driveway. "Mom, speaking as your lawyer, I have to say that Eva's correct. The best thing for you right now would be to turn yourself in. The longer you put it off, the deeper you're digging your hole." He sounded more serious than ever. "I can drive you right down to the police station, and you can make your confession."

"I hope you don't expect me to turn myself in right here and now. I haven't even had breakfast, and my hair's a mess."

With the new haircut and shade of red, she looked like she'd just come from the salon, and judging from the look of her face, she was probably one of those women who slept in her makeup. "I think you look lovely," I said, promising myself that

171

this was the first and only compliment I would ever give her. "And I'm pretty sure they'll provide breakfast—or at least lunch—at the county jail."

"Thanks, honey," she said. "I think we're going to get along really well from here on out. I mean, what could be better than having your mother-in-law locked away in prison?"

Since Grant was still stopped, I took the opportunity to climb over the back seat, planning to sit closer to a door, where I could escape, but as I climbed on top of the seats, I caught a better glimpse of the front seat. Candace was holding a handgun.

So much for moving to the middle seat. In a split second, I had hopped back in the trunk area and was shivering under my blanket as Candace continued her chatter in the front seat. "I really would like to have seen Sophia before I retired."

There she was talking about retiring again, but, by now, I knew it was a ruse. She wasn't planning to turn herself in to the police. She had a gun on Grant, and I didn't doubt that she would shoot him.

"I'll show you how to get to the police station," she said, emphasizing the words police and station as if they were code for something else. We were being hijacked—or kidnapped. She was kidnapping me again! This time, though, I was going to get away.

CHAPTER 23

Candace had a gun on Grant. He was driving, so he couldn't easily take it away from her. That meant I had to do something. But what could I do? I didn't have a phone to call for help, and, except for my belt, I didn't have a weapon. I was stuck behind the back seats of the SUV.

In desperation, I opened up the compartment to my left. I found some jumper cables, some duct tape, and a tire iron. "What are you doing back there?" Candace called. She must have heard me.

Without responding, I weighed the tire iron in my hand. It could have been useful, but I'd have to be closer to Candace if I wanted to use it on her, and there was no way I was crawling over the back seat again.

I looped my wrist through the roll of duct tape, wearing it like a bangle. Then I opened the smaller compartment on the right side of the car. That's when I hit the jackpot. Inside, I found a small fire extinguisher. It wasn't much bigger than a jumbo-size can of hairspray, but the gauge showed it was full.

I read the directions on the back of the extinguisher, trying my best to focus as Candace droned on about her retirement. I had never used a fire extinguisher. I'd never even been around to see anyone else use one. That's how charmed my life had been up until the last week. But the directions didn't make it seem so hard. Just squeeze the trigger hard enough to break the ziptie, aim the hose, and imagine Candace's face was a huge grease fire.

As quietly as I could, I popped up from behind the back seat, catching Grant's eye in the rearview mirror. I held the extinguisher behind the backseat, squeezing the trigger for all I was worth, trying to break that stupid zip tie. You'd think, since my life depended on breaking it, I could have done it in an instant. But my hand strength was just that weak. I clamped my jaws and gave it every ounce of strength. Nope. Nothing. The thing wouldn't break. What kind of idiot thought it was a good idea to put a zip tie on a fire extinguisher anyway?

Candace glanced back at me. "You look frustrated, honey. Anything I can help you with?"

That did it. Her words gave me that extra surge of angst I needed to break through the plastic, and just like that, white powder was flying out the end of the hose onto the ceiling of the car. As fast as I could, I aimed it at Candace's face.

"Stop!" she screamed. "Get it out of my eyes!"

The car slowed and swerved a bit as Grant yanked the gun from her hands.

"How could you do this to me?" Candace spat out foam as she spoke. "I'm your mother."

I crawled over the backseat, still aiming at her. I was going to spray that thing for as long as it lasted. The container said it wasn't toxic, so what was the harm? And what was the harm if it was?

Grant slowed the car even more as he pointed the gun at his own mother. There was no one else on the road. I could tell the extinguisher was giving out as well. The white powder was coming out in spurts now instead of in a powerful stream.

Now that I was in the middle seat, I dropped the extinguisher and grabbed Candace's hands as Grant came to a stop. "Duct tape," I yelled, passing Grant the tape with my free hand.

He followed my cue and without missing a beat was rolling duct tape around his mom's wrists. "You are going to pay for this, Grant," she cried. "Are you even going to get this stuff off my face?"

"It's nontoxic," I said. "No worries."

As soon as his mom was wrapped up, he passed me the gun. "I never thought to ask before if you knew how to use a gun, but you were pretty good back there in the living room. I should have guessed since you grew up in the country—"

"Yeah," I said, completely lying. I'd always hated guns. "Been shooting since I was a toddler. I won the sharpshooting championship last summer." I hoped that was what it was called. My brothers were way more into that stuff than I ever was. The truth was, I was terrified of shooting anyone, even Candace, but with all the powder in her eyes, she couldn't see my hand shaking as I held the gun on her.

Grant began driving again. I estimated that we were still at least fifteen minutes from the police station in West Yellowstone—at least I thought that's where the station would be. I didn't dare ask in case Grant didn't know either. Best pretend both of us knew what we were doing.

"I never cooked you that alligator meat in the fridge," Candace said, which wasn't at all what I expected her to say. "You'll be sure to use it when you get back home? I was saving it just for you." She lifted her taped hands and tried her best to wipe the powder from her face with her sleeve.

"Yes, Mom," Grant said, daring to smirk at me through the rearview mirror.

I rolled my eyes. There was no way I was going anywhere near that alligator meat ... or anything else in that refrigerator. She'd probably poisoned it all before she'd gotten in the car with us.

"I was planning to take you to that new Chinese place in town. Do you suppose they'd be open for brunch?"

"We're not going to brunch." Grant spoke through his teeth.

"Well, we'll have to go somewhere." Candace continued trying to wipe her face with the side of her sleeve. "I can't go to the police station without anything in my stomach."

I responded before Grant had a chance. "I'll bring anything you want to the station—American, Mexican, Chinese, whatever we can find around West Yellowstone. You can eat it right there at the station without having to stay out any longer in this cold air." I wasn't giving her any more opportunities to escape than she already had.

"Uh oh," Grant muttered.

I followed his gaze to see a couple of cars blocking the road ahead of us. It had to be Ronald and Paulo. Candace had probably told them to do this before she got in the car.

Grant slowed the car on the little country road and began to turn around when another car squealed to a stop behind us. I thought it might be just another random car on the highway until I saw the driver—Ingrid. With snow piled high on either side of the road, we were trapped. Grant had no choice but to stop the car.

I kept the gun aimed at Candace. That would give us the most leverage. Not that I could bring myself to pull the trigger.

She placed her hand on Grant's arm. "Don't worry, honey, they won't kill you in front of me."

They wouldn't kill him. What about me?

I hadn't gotten a chance to run last time these people kidnapped me. This time, I had a clear path right between the two cars ahead of us. The door beside me was unlocked.

The dark-tinted window on one of the cars ahead of us rolled down a crack, and I just knew someone was going to stick a gun out.

Our only hope now was for one of us to get help. It was now or never.

"I'm out of here," I told Grant, handing him the gun.

"Go fast," he said, "I'll catch up when I can."

I burst out the side door as the wind whipped my hair into my face. My feet slipped on the icy road, but I made my way to a patch of powdery snow in the middle of the road. I didn't bother to watch our enemies. I watched the road as my feet raced forward. I only looked at the two cars blocking the road long enough to squeeze my way between them.

It was midmorning, and the sun reflected off the snow around me, blinding me with its glare. I estimated it was a fifteen-minute drive until the small country road met the bigger road that led to West Yellowstone.

I hated to leave Grant there by himself, but logically, this was the best thing. Not only was I relieving him of the need to take care of me, I was creating a distraction. Plus, I might also find someone who could help. Please let there be someone who could help—a car driving along the road, someone walking their dog, a lonely old lady cooped up in a cabin with an arsenal of semi-automatic weapons.

Ronald, Paulo, and Ingrid didn't seem to be too distracted by my slipping and sliding past them, though. I ran at least a

176

hundred yards without any of them following me. They seemed much more interested in taking Grant down. Perhaps Candace had told them how little I knew about their crimes. It was more likely, though, that Grant was doing something to distract them from shooting at me. I hoped it wasn't anything too dangerous for him.

Scanning the land around, all I could see was snow and forest. Ronald had probably picked this place because there weren't any houses or businesses for miles. All the more need for me to keep running. Someone had to come driving along the road sooner or later.

Bang! A shot pounded in my ears and then echoed off the hills beside me.

Grant! Was he okay?

I turned back, desperate to know. If he wasn't okay, those people were all going to pay for it.

Candace had promised she wouldn't let them kill him. Not that her promises were worth anything. For all I knew, she might shoot him herself. Good thing he had the gun.

From what I could see, nothing had changed. The two cars still blocked the road, and everyone was still in their cars. Surely, if they'd shot Grant, someone would have gotten out of their car.

I turned back to run down the road. It was then I noticed a small, gray drone hovering above me. It followed me as I raced down the road. When I moved to the right, it moved along with me. When I moved to the left, it followed. One of Candace's people was using a drone to track me. There was no other explanation.

Had anyone ever been injured by a drone? An hour ago, the idea would have seemed laughable. The drone my brothers flew around our farm was flimsy and delicate—more like a remote-control toy than a weapon. It might have broken if it hit me in the head. This drone, though, was much more substantial, and it seem to be on a kamikaze mission to take me down.

I picked up a rock from the side of the road and hurled it at the drone, slipping a little on the ice as I threw. I hit it too, but not enough to do any damage. I only got the edge of the arm, causing it to lose altitude. It recovered, though, before I could find another

177

rock, and it came right at me, buzzing inches from the top of my head like bats sometimes did at night on our farm.

I bent down, running as fast as I could to get away from it, but it buzzed right after me. It was as if the thing wanted revenge for my trying to hit it with a rock.

As it turned and sped toward me again, I turned in the opposite direction with my hands over my head. I'd once heard that if someone was shooting at you, it was best to run in a zig-zag pattern, so I did just that, shuffling first to the right then to the left. Still, the drone dove for me, missing my head by inches. Grant must have still been putting up a fight. Otherwise, they'd all be after me instead of just sending the drone. Sparing a glance back up the road, I saw no sign that anyone had moved from their cars. Everything remained at a standstill.

I could slip and slide in a zig-zag pattern all the way to West Yellowstone if I had to, and this thing could chase me all it wanted. It couldn't kill me. Most likely.

I knelt to pick up another few rocks. Next time it got close, I'd pelt it.

Whoever was driving the thing was good, turning and twisting it to track me as if I were wearing a homing device. I wasn't, was I? I looked down for a split second at my clothes, and the drone took full advantage of my distraction. It dove.

As it did, I chucked one rock after another at it, missing every time. It was enough, though, that the drone missed me by several feet. Ha! Foiled again.

I kept running as the drone turned and flew back toward the cars. It probably needed its battery charged by now. If it was anything like my brothers' drone, that would take at least ten minutes.

My feet skated down the road as my chest heaved. I had to keep up speed now that I didn't have to think about the drone. This was my chance to put some distance between us.

I saw no cars on the road ahead—no one I could flag down to call the police. We were too far out of town. The wind howled around me, blowing snow across the asphalt and into my face. Still, I scooted along, even as the drifted snow reached my ankles.

Where were Mr. Tilney and Sophia? Surely they could guess we needed help by now, and it wasn't like this town had all that many roads where they could search for us. If they didn't want to drive out here themselves, they could at least call the police. Better yet, Mr. Tilney had friends at the airport. He could search for us by helicopter. Maybe that was his plan.

But when I glanced above me, all I saw was the drone hovering high above me—it had returned. A hatch opened in its underside and something dropped out—something round and green.

CHAPTER 24

My instincts shouted to run for the side of the road, and I launched myself into a bank of snow. As I sank into the snow, a deafening explosion shocked my eardrums. They'd tried to drop a bomb on me.

I held my hands over my ears as a shower of debris rained down. It had to have been a bomb—or maybe a grenade.

If this was what they were doing to me, what were they doing to Grant? I had to get help, and I needed to get it fast.

I took off running down the road again, sparing a glance to see where the grenade had hit. A star of black streaks marked the spot—a much larger spot than I'd ever seen after our Fourth of July fireworks parties. There was also a pothole in the road that I was sure wasn't there before.

Once again, I could not believe this was happening to me. I wasn't the type to hold a gun on someone or to get chased by a drone.

It was probably just as well that I couldn't believe it was happening. Disbelief was better than being paralyzed by fear, and the worst thing that could happen right then was to let fear get the better of me.

I had to keep slipping and sliding up the road.

If I could just get through this, I promised myself, I would never leave my family's country farm again. Grant had to get through it too, though. I couldn't go on, knowing he'd died.

I scanned the woods again for houses and the road ahead for cars, but it was all snow and forest. All I could do was keep running. I slid along as fast as I could, and as I did, I prayed that a vehicle would come along soon. Even if whoever was inside could just call the police for me. They didn't need to let me in the car— I probably looked horrifying with all the fake blood dying the front of my white coat. This was an emergency, though, and people out here in the Montana wilderness were likely to come to the rescue of a wounded girl. Maybe the fake blood was an asset.

The snow started to fall again—lightly, but I hoped that would be enough to ground the stupid drone.

Apparently not. The drone was right above me. Before I could get away, the hatch on its bottom opened, and another grenade dropped.

I ran as fast as I could, but I didn't stand a chance. The grenade was so close, it clattered to the asphalt right in front of me. I saw it in detail as I hopped over it. It was like the grenades I'd seen in movies, only rounder and dark green with a wire ring near the top.

I expected it to blast at any second. One, two, three. The farther away I could get, the better.

By the time I'd counted to twenty, it still hadn't gone off. Images of maimed soldiers flashed through my mind.

When I got to fifty, I turned and looked back. Had I not heard it explode? Strange. The last one had exploded as soon as it hit the ground.

Something had to be wrong. Was it a dud?

Then I remembered seeing the wire ring near the top. Wasn't that part attached to the pin? Those idiots had forgotten to pull the pin! I'd seen it right there in front of me.

Thank you, God! I'd been spared. I was still alive and whole with every part of my body intact.

I ran another fifty steps before I realized I could use that grenade! I didn't know how, but I had the feeling it was the find of a lifetime. With the pin intact, it would be safe enough for me to pick up. In the movies, soldiers carried them around in their pockets. Besides, it wasn't safe to leave it there on the street.

I doubled back, counting to a hundred again as I searched for a spot of green in the snow. The way back was downhill, and I hoped I wasn't sacrificing the time for something I didn't really need. Still, the grenade would be protection—something to have on hand in case Ronald or Paulo came after me. All I had to do was pull the pin and throw. It would explode on impact.

I could use it if I needed to go back to rescue Grant. How, I didn't know. Throw it under Ronald's car? That would surely kill him. I didn't want to kill anyone, but if it meant saving Grant, it was what I needed to do.

What about the drone, though? Someone could see everything I did through the drone's camera. They would know I had the grenade. If this was going to work, I had to take the drone down for good before I picked up the grenade.

As I waited for the drone to return, I gathered some rocks from the side of the road, stuffing them one after another into my pockets. I also piled a few at my feet. Then I waited, standing still on the side of the road.

When it came into sight, I aimed a few feet ahead of it and threw. The rock went too far ahead of the drone. The next throw went too far behind. I threw five more times without hitting, wishing that it would fly close enough for me to reach out and grab it.

I could hit it with a rock. I just needed to focus. The drone was almost directly above me now, which meant that I was likely to get hit in the head by the rocks I threw up at it. I ran faster, trying to get out from under it. Then, taking a chance that it wouldn't follow me into the forest, I stepped off the road. I lunged knee-deep in snow, leaping through the white powder as fast as I could as I weaved around trees and brush, which turned out to be not that fast at all. It took about ten times as long to take a step, and the drone followed me just as closely as it did on the road, buzzing around the branches.

I guessed the drone was about to open its little hatch and drop another grenade—this time with the pin pulled. There was no way I'd get away in time with two feet of snow around my legs. Going into the woods had been a mistake. I'd have to give up on hitting the drone with a rock and go back to the road. I pivoted and, as soon as I did, I heard a crash above me.

The drone must have hit a tree. But I didn't stop to see for sure. I ran for my life.

An explosion sounded. I covered my ears and kept running, but as I stepped back onto the street, my feet slipped on the snow, and I fell forward, scraping my hands on the pavement.

Behind me, branches broke and a tree thudded to the ground. The smell of scorched plastic filled the air.

When things grew quiet, I dared to search the sky for any sign of the drone. Nothing.

I couldn't tell for sure, but chances were good that I was free from the drone.

I was free to rescue Grant.

I backtracked along the road until I found the grenade that hadn't exploded. My eyes hadn't tricked me. It did have the pin still attached. I wasn't sure what I was going to do with it, but I had seen that it could cause damage as far away as twenty feet. Wherever I threw it, it had to be at least twenty feet away from Grant.

I cradled it against my chest as I slid down the road. If I remembered correctly, the cars were parked about a half mile away. I couldn't see exactly how far away because the road had curved a bit.

The fact that none of the bad guys had come looking for me gave me hope that Grant was still keeping them busy. Now I just had to come up with a plan.

When I got to the curve in the road, I stepped back into the deep snow along the side of the road and began walking through the forest again. This way would be slower, but I could hide behind evergreens and tree trunks as I approached our enemies.

My legs ached from all the exercise. Walking through the snow was harder on my leg muscles than I'd anticipated. As for my arms, I'd already figured out from trying to throw rocks at the drone that they weren't up to the task of throwing the grenade either.

I weighed the green ball in my hand, trying to pretend it was simply a rock. How did Candace's people even get a hold of a grenade or learn how to use them in drones? It probably had something to do with all their trade in South America.

My only advantage was that I'd seen plenty of old movies. All I had to do was pull the pin, throw it, and then run in the opposite direction. How hard could it be? If I could throw a rock, I could throw a grenade. My aim didn't have to be all that good.

Still, my hands shook as I looked down at the metal ring. How did I know the grenade was the same as the others that exploded on impact. This one could be set to explode through an electronic signal. I held it to my ear, wondering if grenades ever ticked like bombs. I heard nothing, which I took as a good sign. How I wished I could call Mr. Tilney for advice. He probably knew all about grenades and road blocks, or at least he could search the internet for me as I trudged.

Coming out from around a huge evergreen, I caught sight of the cars blocking the road ahead of me. They were still a thousand feet or so down the road.

I moved forward, little by little, keeping low and hiding behind trees and bushes. I saw no movement around the cars, and I wondered again about the gunshot I'd heard. It didn't appear that anyone had been hurt, at least that I could see.

I snuck closer and closer until I could see Ronald and Paulo sitting in their cars. They were both talking on their phones and didn't appear to have noticed me. I could throw the grenade right at them, and they wouldn't see it coming. But I wasn't sure if it would be too close to Grant.

I could make out the top of the SUV that Grant was driving, but I couldn't tell if he and Candace were still inside.

I didn't dare move any closer. It was best to attack by surprise—before anyone noticed me. Still, the prospect of throwing the grenade worried me. A grenade explosion too close to Ronald's car could set off a deadly gas fire for everyone around. My safest choice was either to use the grenade as a distraction or a threat, and frankly, I wasn't feeling brave enough to walk out and threaten anyone with a grenade. It was going to have to be a distraction.

I snuck through the woods until I had a clear area for my throw. Then I pulled the pin and hurled the grenade about fifteen feet down the road from Ronald's car.

It exploded as soon as it hit the asphalt—on impact—and I took advantage of the distraction to race through the woods until I got to a place where I could see if Grant was okay. It wouldn't be hard for Ronald and Paulo to find me. I'd left plenty of tracks

184

through the snow, and I no longer had a weapon to protect myself, except those few rocks that were still in my pockets. My hands were shaking so much, I wasn't sure I could even grip one of them.

I stopped behind an evergreen and peeked through the branches to see that Grant was still behind the wheel of the SUV, his gun pointing at Candace, who was talking on her phone. If Grant had seen me, he wasn't letting on to it. Ronald had gotten out of his car while Paulo was eyeing the woods.

Ronald ran his hand along the side of the car. "Whatever it was, the paint job is ruined." He looked up in the air. "And I'm gonna need a new windshield. If I didn't know better ..." He looked up again, as if he were searching for the drone. "If I didn't know better, I'd say it was a grenade. What are you up to, Grant?" Paulo yelled. "You got someone else helping you?"

Ingrid walked up to him. "I say we kill him. Then we drive down the road and get the girl."

I didn't stop to think. With one fluid motion, I reached into my pocket, grabbed a rock, and flung it at her. Unlike every other throw I'd made that day, this one hit exactly where I aimed, Ingrid's hand. She dropped the gun, exclaiming in pain. Ronald bent to pick it up, but before he could reach it, Grant was out of the SUV, pointing the gun at them. "Hands behind your heads or I'll shoot," he called.

They put their hands behind their heads as he took Ronald's gun from his pocket and then placed a foot on Ingrid's gun. "Get in the SUV," he commanded, his voice loud and strong, "now."

A shot rang out. And then another. Grant fell. Or did he duck behind the car? I couldn't see him.

I gripped another rock in my pocket and looked for Paulo. All I could see was a gun pointing out his window.

I flung another rock, hitting his car square in the windshield, cracking it. At the same time, another shot rang out.

"That's enough!" Candace shrieked, leaping out of the car with her hands still duct-taped together. "I don't care what he's done. If any of you hurt my son, I'll have your heads." She walked up to Paulo's car, snatched the gun away with her duct-taped hands and pointed it at him.

On the other side of the car, Grant stood. He was okay, and I could breathe again. "Thanks, Mom." He still pointed the gun at Ingrid and Ronald.

Candace had been true to her word. She had protected Grant. But I still wasn't sure I could trust her.

In the distance, a siren sounded. Someone must have heard all the noise and called the police. It was about time.

I let Grant wait with the bad guys on the road while I stayed hidden behind the trees, ready to throw a rock if Candace turned the gun on Grant. Every minute felt like an hour, as I knelt in the snow, praying that the police would come faster.

It must have taken a full five minutes from the time I first heard the siren for the police to arrive. And only one officer came—a guy who looked to be a few years past retirement. He parked his car perpendicular to Ronald's, got out, and pulled his gun, pointing it at Grant. "Put down your weapon."

Grant did as he was told, placing his gun and then the other guns on the street before raising his hands in the air. "I can explain everything, and it might help if we put a call in to the U.S. Office of Fish and Wildlife."

"Just hold your horses," the officer called. "All of you, face down on the ground. Hands behind your backs."

Ronald muttered something in a foreign language while Candace curled her top lip. "In the snow?" she asked.

"Now!" the officer yelled, and they did exactly as they were told.

The officer pulled out his radio. "This is Jim. I'm gonna need some backup on state road 293. This is turning out to be a whole lot more than a few teenagers setting off fireworks."

I expected that the dispatcher would have told Officer Jim that Grant was a good guy since Mr. Tilney was probably in touch with them. But it didn't appear that Jim knew anything about the situation. He stood over Grant, pointing the gun at his head.

Now that the officer had control of all the guns, I made my way past the big evergreen tree and through the snow and bushes until I reached the road. I didn't want to surprise the officer, so I called out. "Hi, I don't have a gun or anything. I just came down to explain—"

"—Stay where you are," Officer Jim shouted without even looking my way. "Keep your hands in the air."

"These people," I explained, "all except the guy in the blue shirt—kidnapped me and tried to kill me. The man in the blue shirt is the good guy. They want to kill him too."

Candace heaved a sigh but stayed face down on the asphalt. "Officer, I've been a law-abiding citizen of this town for ten years now. My neighbors can tell you I wouldn't harm a fly."

"But she would harm exotic animals," I said. "You should pay a visit to her basement. She has all sorts of monkeys and birds she brought here illegally."

"So I'm an animal lover," Candace said, lifting her head to look at the officer. "What's the harm in that?"

"The harm is that over half of them die in transport," Grant said, his voice calm, "and that people are starting to get hurt as well. I thought we agreed you were going to turn yourself in."

Another police car pulled to a stop behind Ingrid's car, and a young female officer got out, her gun also pointed at Grant. "What have we got here, Jim?"

"Some sort of altercation," Jim said. "We're going to take them all in. But before we do that, we'll need to get these cars out of the way. Old Mrs. Benson is liable to drive right into this blockade, especially if the snow gets any heavier."

The officer recited our Miranda rights and began cuffing everyone, starting with Grant and ending with me. "You all right?" she asked, eyeing the stains on the front of my jacket. Her badge read Stark.

"Yeah," I said, "it's fake blood."

Officer Stark raised an eyebrow. "Into the car, then." She led me to her squad car, where I squeezed into the back seat beside Candace and Grant. Candace sat in the middle.

"You and Grant make such a nice couple," Candace said in a sickly-sweet tone. "I just hope he's a better husband than he is a son." I felt sorry for Grant when she said that, but I ended up feeling even sorrier for Mr. Tilney. Ten years of marriage with that sort of manipulation would have made even Santa Clause grumpy. And that, in turn, made me feel even sorrier for Grant, growing up with a manipulative mother and a grumpy father.

I couldn't keep the anger from my voice. "He's a great son, and I'm sure he'll be a great husband to whoever is lucky enough to marry him."

She lifted a brow at me and then shook her head as she watched Officer Jim getting into Ronald's car to move it to the side of the road. "Oh, honey, what I wouldn't give to be so sweet and young again. Naiveté is so good for the psyche."

I didn't respond. She was only trying to wound me, and I wasn't about to let her. Instead, I leaned forward to speak to Grant. "What was that shot I heard after I escaped?"

Grant watched the police officers out the window. "Paulo was getting out of his car to follow you," he said, his voice low. "I decided he needed some incentive to stay put."

After the officers moved the cars that were blocking the road, we drove all the way into West Yellowstone. There were no more road blocks. No drones. No grenades. Just a little dusting of snow. This was what Grant had been working so hard for all these months. Here Candace was about to turn herself in and mend her ways. She looked happy, that fake kind of happy she'd been trying to pull off for the last twenty minutes. But Grant just looked tired.

I spoke again when we pulled into the parking lot behind the tiny police station and several officers came to escort us from the car. They would be my parting words to Candace, the last thing I ever wanted to say to her. "I hope you'll remember your promise to confess what you've done."

"I'll make sure you get a fair sentence," Grant said.

She faced straight ahead without looking at either of us. "I can handle this myself."

"Okay?" Grant said, like it was a question, and the hurt in his voice matched the pain in his eyes. She was betraying his trust again.

We walked inside as a group, each of us accompanied by an officer. My officer, a young red-headed man, couldn't stop looking at me. "Are you okay, ma'am?"

That's when I remembered the blood. "Oh, yeah," I said, shrugging as best I could with my hands cuffed. "It's fake. I'm fine."

In front of me, Candace stood tall and straight, gazing down on her officer as if she were the Queen of England. "I can explain everything. My son and his girlfriend are trying to frame me for crimes they committed. Have you ever heard of elder abuse?"

"I'd like to call a lawyer," Grant said.

That's when I knew that proving our innocence wasn't going to be as easy as I'd thought.

CHAPTER 25

While we waited for our lawyers to arrive, Candace explained everything the police needed to know about Grant's lifetime of elder abuse. According to her, he had made a regular habit of duct-taping her hands and taking her money. And she told Officer Stark all this while Grant and I were sitting right there, in the same little room. That, in itself, should have been a hint to the officer. Candace wasn't the least bit scared of Grant.

"I'll show her elder abuse," I whispered under my breath as Officer Stark took detailed notes of everything Candace told him.

Grant didn't laugh. He was probably too nervous. "If we could talk to the U.S. Fish and Wildlife Office in Denver," he told the police officer, "they can help me explain what this is all about. My mother's been trafficking illegal animals for over a decade, and I've got evidence on my phone." Unfortunately, with his hands in cuffs, he wasn't able to get his phone out and show her.

Officer Stark turned back to her laptop. "Hmm." I guessed that she had never had to deal with an alleged case of elder abuse and animal abuse all in the same family and all in one day.

While she called in a doctor to examine Candace for signs of abuse, I called Mr. Tilney to bring me a change of clothes. He answered the phone on the first ring and then showed up within minutes—right after the doctor and another female officer took Candace into an examining room. Meanwhile, Ingrid, Ronald, and Paulo were still pretending they couldn't speak English or Spanish. The officers thought they might be speaking Arabic and had called in a translator.

Grant's knee bounced up and down as he glanced at the clock on the wall. "I hope you're going to keep an eye on my mother while she's with the doctor," he told the officer.

Officer Stark nodded as she continued making notes on her laptop. "I've got another officer in the hallway."

"If you need any evidence against Candace," Mr. Tilney told Officer Stark, "I've still got a freezer full of the meat she imported illegally."

The officer stared at him, her mouth slightly open.

I scooted to the edge of my seat. "You mean the freezer out in the garage, the one with the brass lock?"

Mr. Tilney pointed at me. "That's the one. The meat in it may be fourteen years old, but it's got her fingerprints all over it."

I'd been right all along. There was something odd about that freezer, though I doubted a police officer in Montana would be able to do anything about a freezer in Oklahoma. We'd have to wait for the federal agents to take care of it. "Is anyone going to call the Fish and Wildlife Office?" I whispered to Grant while the officer continued to type into her laptop.

Grant shook his head.

"Where is Candace anyway?" Mr. Tilney asked the officer.

The officer pointed a thumb down the hallway. "In the examination room."

Mr. Tilney raised an eyebrow. "They'd better be careful. She's liable to escape at any moment."

The officer simply nodded as she continued to type. "Officer Ray knows what she's doing."

"Maybe it would help if we took you to see the evidence," I told Officer Stark. "There are monkeys, parrots, crocodiles, and leopards. You really should see it for yourself."

"I'm afraid exotic animals aren't my jurisdiction," Officer Stark said.

I wished I had something on these people that didn't have anything to do with exotic animals. What else could I tell them about Candace?

"I've got a report on file in Texas about how Ronald and Ingrid kidnapped me," I said. Still, though, it was the same old story. I really had no proof of the kidnapping—no photos, videos, or fingerprints. All I'd had was Candace's purse and her car.

"I'll look into that," the officer said, giving me a quick glance while typing her report.

It was such a strange thing that Ronald and Candace happened to be driving stolen cars that day. Perhaps they made a habit of it. "What about stolen cars?" I asked the officer. "Is that your jurisdiction?"

"We already ran all the plates from the cars blocking the road. They checked out fine."

I looked at Grant, who shrugged. "Ronald told me it's too much of a hassle to steal a car in Montana," he said.

Mr. Tilney was still on the phone with the U.S. Fish and Wildlife Division in Denver. It sounded like they were sending a federal agent, but it was going to be a few hours before he arrived. "Can you have someone call the police down here and let them know how Grant's been working with you?" Mr. Tilney asked. Then he paused listening. "Okay. That sounds good."

Grant leaned toward me. "I don't have a good feeling about this."

"She's down," an officer called in the hallway. I leaned forward to see out the door. Candace was lying on the ground, her limbs trembling. She was faking a seizure. The doctor rolled his eyes at the officer. I cringed. Didn't Candace know that sort of thing was politically incorrect?

Mr. Tilney bared his teeth and marched out to where Candace lay. He stared down at her. "If you ever want Sophia to visit you," he yelled, "you'd better quit this nonsense right now."

That stopped Candace cold. She lay still, moaning. "What did you say?" she asked, her eyes still closed.

Mr. Tilney repeated himself. "Sophia and I have talked about it. She says she'll only come visit you when you're behind bars."

Her eyes fluttered open. "You mean I could see my darling Sophia today?" she asked. "If I got myself in jail?"

Officer Ray tilted her head to the side, her eyes narrowing. "I'd say it's highly likely you'll get your wish."

Was it possible Candace cared that much about Sophia, or was this another one of her tricks? I watched her the way I would watch a coyote that was hanging around the chicken coop. Sophia needed to know the truth about her mom, but I wasn't sure one meeting at a jail would do it for her. The woman was too good of an actress.

"I didn't actually know what I was doing was a crime," Candace said. "I'm not the kind of person who would intentionally do something wrong. I did it all for the love of God's creatures. When I lived in Mexico, I became accustomed to keeping some of the jungle animals as pets, so I didn't see any harm in bringing them with me when I came back to the states."

I expected Grant to offer an alternate explanation, but he kept his mouth shut as his mother continued to talk. As it turned out, his was a good strategy. The more Candace talked, detailing the benefits of owning endangered animals, the wider the officers' eyes became.

"Take the case of the jaguar," Candace said. "They used to be spread all over North and South America, but humans have taken over their habitat, and now they only exist in pocket populations. Those of us who are more conservation-minded are happy to bring them into our homes and breed them in captivity. We only want to ensure the survival of the species. That's why I do what I do."

I was about to challenge her argument, but Officer Jim approached us with a paper in his hand. "Ms. Tilney, I've got a warrant for your arrest from Texas."

I remembered what Sophia had said about Grant clearing my case with the police in Texas. Officer Jim hadn't said anything about a warrant for my arrest—so far.

Candace, who was still sitting on the floor after her fake seizure, blinked a few times. "A warrant for me?"

"For you," Officer Jim said, a hint of amusement in his voice, as he lifted her by the elbow to stand up.

She shook her head as she stood beside the officer. "There has to be some mistake."

He looked over the papers. "No mistake. In fact, we've got warrants for your three friends as well."

He began pulling her in the direction of the holding cell, but she turned back to speak to Mr. Tilney. "Do you really think Sophia will come visit me?"

193

"I'll have to ask her," Mr. Tilney said, frowning in the same way he'd frowned on the same night Grant brought me to his house. "If it were up to me, you'd never see her."

"But you said she wanted to see me," Candace said. "She wanted to see me when I was in jail."

"Or prison," Mr. Tilney said, "There'll be plenty of time for that."

Several other officers escorted Ingrid, Ronald, and Paulo in the same direction, taking them through a heavy door.

I couldn't help jumping up in triumph as the door slammed behind them. We had succeeded. Grant had completed his mission, and we were both still alive. I was free to return to my life as a community college student in rural Texas, only it wouldn't be quite so boring now that Grant was in the picture.

I grinned at Grant. while Officer Stark removed the zipties from my wrists and then from Grant's. "You're free to go," she told us, "but stay close by. The federal agents from Denver want to talk to you when they arrive in town."

Mr. Tilney looked at his watch. "I'd better head back to the hotel and let Sophia know what's happened."

That left Grant and me alone for the first time in over a week.

"I'm starving," Grant said as we leaped down the front steps of the station. "What do you feel like eating?"

"Anything but alligator," I responded, "but don't we have to take care of all those animals in your mom's basement first? The agent won't be coming to get them for another few hours."

"Spoken like a true farm girl," Grant said. "But you have to remember that we don't have a car at the moment. There's no reason to worry about the animals, though. Ronald and Paulo fed them this morning. They can last another few hours." When we got to the sidewalk, we turned toward the tourist district in the center of town.

"Is there a restaurant around here that serves spectacular desserts?" I asked. "You still haven't kept that part of the bargain." I looked down at the pair of jeans and sweatshirt that Mr. Tilney had brought for me to change into. I wasn't dressed for anything

194

too fancy. Of course, I didn't expect there'd be anything like that in West Yellowstone.

He reached for my hand. "Well, there is a place that's famous for their pie, but you deserve a lot more than pie after all I've put you through. Besides that, I said, 'until dessert do us part.' I'm nowhere near ready to part."

I smiled up at him. "Well, we can make a new vow, like, 'until the one hundred thousandth dessert do us part.'"

"I'll agree to that," he said, "as long as you don't keep count."

I wasn't in any hurry for our dessert pact to end either, especially now that everything was getting resolved with the police. "You've got a deal."

He stopped right there on the sidewalk and leaned down to kiss me, sending me into the most comforting sense of déjà vu I'd ever experienced. The touch of his lips seemed so familiar and somehow that made it all the more exciting. We belonged together, and now we were getting that chance.

"Thank you for everything," he said, running his finger down the side of my face. "You saved my life—really, you have no idea. I came out here to Montana, intending to finish what I started, but I realized when I got here that if Ronald had anything to do with it, I wouldn't make it out alive. And if Ronald didn't kill me, Paulo would."

So they would've killed Grant if I hadn't come. I bit the side of my lip, knowing it was time for my apology. "I'm so sorry I blew your cover at that truck stop. It's my fault that you were in so much danger."

He shook his head. "If we're going to argue about who's at fault, I'm going to win. I was the one who saw a beautiful woman at the diner and decided to sit by her. That's how all this started, but I can't say I'm sorry that I did it." He grinned, and I caught my breath. He may have had a terrible mother, but at least she passed down some good looks to him. I'd have to thank his dad later for teaching him honesty and integrity.

We walked through the small town until we came to a restaurant that looked like a log cabin—well, except for the parking lot and sign out front with "Lou's" written in large red letters.

It was 3:15 in the afternoon, and I saw no cars in the parking lot. "Do you think they're open?" I asked. It wasn't tourist season yet.

"With the luck we're having today," he said, squeezing my hand, "of course they'll be open."

Sure enough, a server stood ready to greet us when we arrived.

The inside of the place kept to the cabin theme perfectly. Dark-colored log walls surrounded us. A few deer antler chandeliers hung from the ceiling while light streamed in through the windows. In the background, I heard a hint of piano music. "Can we please sit near the fireplace?" Grant asked, gesturing toward the huge rock fireplace on the other side of the room, where a fire blazed.

I'd always wanted to sit in a cabin by a fireplace like the one in *White Christmas*.

"Right this way," the server said, grabbing a couple of menus.

We sat across from each other at the small, circular table that stood just to the left of the fireplace while the girl recited the day's specials. I couldn't pay attention to her, though. I was too busy wondering if this could be a dream. It seemed too good to be true. The crisis was finally over, and we were sitting down to have a nice, normal date.

"So what are your plans now that all this is over?" I asked after the server left us to look over the menu.

"I was thinking I might like to be a lawyer in a small town in Texas." He winked.

Nice. I was dating a lawyer. Not that I'd minded dating a trucker, but there was something about dating a lawyer that sounded so posh. "That's funny," I said. "I was thinking it might be fun to move to the city, where it's easier for lawyers to get jobs."

He leaned in, completely ignoring his menu. "Would you go to college in the city?" The side of his shin brushed against mine.

I walked my fingers toward his hand. "That depends whether a certain lawyer moves to a small town or a city. Up until last week, my grades were good enough to get into most of the state colleges."

"How many days of classes have you missed?"

I had to think about that for a while. "What's today?"

He must have been just as mixed up as I was because he had to pull out his phone to look. "Tuesday, April 10."

I laughed. It had only been ten days since we'd met in the diner although it had seemed so much longer. "I've only missed two days of school then. Actually, I haven't missed my Tuesday classes yet because they're in the afternoon and evening. My first class starts in—" I turned his phone so I could see the time— "five minutes. All my classes are in the late afternoon or evening."

"Well, I'll make sure to get everything straightened out with the federal agents so you can go back by tomorrow afternoon."

I tried for a smile, but the truth was that I was disappointed that our time together would end that soon. "Thank you."

He picked up his menu and started to read it. "They have apple pie ala mode." He dropped the menu onto the table again. "How mad do you think your parents are going to be at me?"

"What do you mean?"

Worry wrinkles appeared around his eyes. "How much have you told them about me taking you in my truck and leaving you at my dad's house?"

I shrugged, guessing his parents got angry at him a lot more than my parents did. I smiled. "So far, they only know what I've told them about you."

"Oh, like how I got you kidnapped and accused of armed robbery?" He raked a hand through his hair. "I'm going to have my work cut out for me in trying to convince them to let me date you."

I sat back, thinking that through. My parents wouldn't blame him for something his mother did, but how would they feel about him pretending to shoot me? I'd better just never mention

197

that part "Well," I said, "I'm just glad you want to date me. And I can't wait for dessert."

CHAPTER 26

I wasn't too happy to be back to Candace's house that night. The only thing that made it better was the fact that we were accompanied by three federal agents, each carrying a gun. Grant took them downstairs and gave them a tour of each room—including the room I never entered that contained a wolf. The agent made friends with him by holding out a dog treat.

After the tour, while the group of agents began to catalog the reptiles, Grant and I went into the next room to start feeding the monkeys. "Here, you take care of the water." He pointed to a sink in the corner. "I'll start on the food. Hopefully, I don't mess it up." He opened the refrigerator to reveal stacks of clear plastic containers, each labeled. "This morning was my first time helping out here, and I was pretty distracted, always having to worry that Ronald might be getting ready to kill me. You heard how he pulled a knife on me in the Granny Annie's parking lot?"

I cringed. "Yeah." Once again, I had to remind myself that Candace and her friends were behind bars. We could think of other things now.

"What's going to happen to all these animals?" I asked as I filled a pitcher at the sink.

Grant took a clear plastic container of fruit out of the refrigerator and opened it as he walked toward the monkeys, who were already reaching through the bars of their crates. "They'll be considered evidence until my mother's case is finished, so they'll probably be held at a nearby zoo or sanctuary. After that, they'll be relocated to other zoos here in the United States." He handed one of the monkeys a piece of apple. "The only possible exception is the wolf in the other room. My mom got him from a farmer in Wyoming. I'm not an expert, but I think there's a chance they'll release him back into the wild."

"So these little monkeys won't ever get back to the jungle?" I'd always thought that would be the end result. I mean, wasn't that the right thing to do? That's where they belonged.

"No. Travel is too hard on these guys. Around half of the animals die during transport—even more than that sometimes if the handlers aren't careful."

"That's so sad."

He heaved a sigh. "One more reason I wanted Mom out of the business. If we can stop people from selling exotic animals, there won't be a reason to take them from their native environments."

He opened the door to the monkey cage and took out a food tray, but before he could fill it up, a golden tamarin escaped, eating a piece of banana from Grant's hand and then crawling onto Grant's shoulders. Grant laughed.

"What a cutie!" I said, coming up to meet the little monkey. I held my arm out and it crawled from Grant's shoulder onto mine, perching itself on top of my head, its little fingers gripping my hair. "I've never held a monkey before."

"They're not good pets," Grant said. "They're meant to live in groups of other monkeys."

"But this one obviously likes people too."

Grant lifted it off my head and let it down to run in circles on the concrete floor. "Yes, he'll be very popular with the zookeepers wherever he ends up, but he won't be as happy as he was before he was captured."

I held out an orange segment for the monkey, which it took. "I wish we knew where all the animals are going to end up. You don't suppose the government would ever tell us, do you?"

"We can ask the agents, but it's not like they'll tell us. My mother was an animal trafficker." Grant finished filling the food tray and put it in the monkey's cage. Then he tried to lure the tamarin inside with a trail of fruit, but the little guy just ran in the opposite direction.

"Your mother may have been a trafficker," I said, filling up the water dish, "but you're a rescuer. Look at all these animals you've saved, and all the ones who'll be safer in the future because of you."

"In the future, I'm going to stick with the kind of rescue where you go down to the shelter and pick out a dog or a cat." He caught the monkey as it ran by him and gently placed it back in its cage. "Now that I'm through trucking, I was thinking I might like a cat … unless you're allergic?"

I grinned. He was asking my opinion, which meant he saw a future for us. "I'm not allergic, but what about Slurpee?"

"Sophia told me a few days ago that she won't let me take him back. She likes having a dog around the house. So what do you think: a dog or a cat?"

"Either one. Just don't get any snakes or lizards."

He smiled and nodded. "No snakes or lizards. Agreed." He swung open the door of the next crate, and the tiny monkey inside escaped.

"Are you going to let all of them escape?"

He shrugged. "If I could, I'd let them all out at once, but I can't be sure they'll get along. These little pygmy marmosets are illegal to export from South America."

The monkey was about the size of my hand. "Does that mean they're endangered?"

"I don't think so, but they could be if they became legal to export. They're a fashionable pet right now. Mom has sold twenty or thirty of them in the last few weeks."

To me, the words fashionable and pet didn't belong together. A monkey could live around twenty years, but fashions only lasted for two or three. What would happen to all the little monkeys after they went out of style? They'd be like the little purse dogs I'd read about—once people realized how much work they were, they were abandoned or sent to a shelter. "It's a good thing you're putting a stop to this, Grant."

"I'm glad you think so. I'm just sorry you had to get involved. I would have never set foot inside that diner if I'd known how much trouble it'd cause you."

I raised an eyebrow and set a hand on my hip. "So you regret setting foot in the diner?"

He stepped closer to me, placing his hands on my shoulders and kissing my forehead. "I didn't say I regret it. I just never intended to put you in danger. I'm sorry we couldn't just go to the police in Texas and resolve everything right then and there, but

201

that would have given my mom the opportunity to hide all the evidence."

I stood on tiptoe to kiss him on the lips. "Maybe you could pay me back by finding me an excellent lawyer."

"The government has already cleared your case with the police, but in case you still have any trouble, I know just the guy, and he'll give you free law services."

"For how long?" I asked.

He slid his hands down to my waist. "Forever."

Forever? That sounded serious. Of course, I deserved it. I had saved his life, after all.

"If you'll take them," he added.

I was going to have to think about that ... for a long, long time.

Epilogue

Since I didn't get a chance to visit Yellowstone during my first whirlwind tour of Montana, Grant took me back there in early fall for our honeymoon. We stayed in a little cabin surrounded by tall pine trees, but our favorite place was a little bend in the river we discovered deep within Yellowstone Park. We parked the car along the side of the road and took off our shoes. Grant rolled up his pants, but my vintage sundress required no adaptation.

We stepped into the shallow waters, which had been warmed to the perfect temperature by a nearby hot spring. Minnows swam past, tickling our ankles as we gazed out on the mountains that surrounded us. It was nature at its most pristine. Grant reached for my hand. "When I first came here, two years ago, I didn't think this place could get any more beautiful, but I was wrong. You have a way of turning every scene into a masterpiece."

I gave his hand a squeeze. "I could say the same thing about you. I never thought that life could be this good."

Grant's law practice had taken off amazingly well in our little Texas town—perhaps because he was the one and only lawyer we'd ever had. Of course, Grant and I still had our problems. His mother being problem number one. She had been kind enough, though, to send us a wedding gift—a jungle scene she painted in her prison cell.

With her mother in prison, Sophia was free to leave the house more often now, and on at least three of those occasions, she'd gone on a date with my brother Wade, who had broken up with Clayton's sister.

Grant put a finger to his lips and pointed down the river.

"What?" I whispered.

"It's a wolf. Can you see it?" I stepped closer to him, so I could see exactly where he was pointing—a spot along the riverbank about a hundred yards upriver. "It's lying down beside that dead tree." I stared at the fallen tree trunk until I saw something move beside it—something that was almost the same color, just whiter.

Grant grabbed our picnic supplies and some binoculars from his car. After spreading a blanket on the grass at a safe distance from the wolf, we sat down to eat some artisan bread, cheese, and grapes Grant had bought in town.

A chill prickled my skin as I stared through the binoculars at the wolf, trying to compare it to my memory from the last year. "What do you suppose the government did with that wolf in your mom's basement?"

Grant took a bite of bread and chewed it before answering. "I never found out." He clearly wasn't experiencing the same sense of familiarity that I was.

But that wolf had come from around Yellowstone. It would have made sense for the agents to release it back into the park. "You don't think this could be the same wolf?" I handed him the binoculars.

He looked through them for a minute and then shook his head. "It's not likely."

"But it is possible."

He took another look through the binoculars. "There are around seventy-five packs of wolves in the park. That's a lot of wolves, Eva, and probably plenty of them are white."

The wolf lay in the sun for a while. Then slowly, it made its way down to the river, wading until it was up to its belly in the water. It splashed around a bit, stooping to drink. Then it wagged its tail and shook off as it climbed back out to sun itself on the log.

I lay next to Grant on the soft grass. Taking into account the feel of his body next to mine, the taste of the food, and the sound of the rippling river, I couldn't imagine a more perfect moment. "Is it possible to be too happy?" I asked.

"I was wondering the same thing last night as I watched you sleep." He leaned over to kiss me softly on the lips.

"You watched me sleep?" Before I'd met Grant, I'd never hoped to receive that kind of admiration from a man, especially not someone as amazing as Grant.

He chuckled as if he found my disbelief amusing. "Yes, and then I looked up on my phone if it's possible to be too happy."

"What did you find?"

"A quote by Jane Austen: 'It is well to have as many holds on happiness as possible.'" He reached for my hand. "And you," he squeezed my hand, "are my number one hold."

TO THE READER

Dear Reader,
You are the reason I write. Thank you for reading this book. If you enjoyed your read, would you please consider leaving a review on Amazon.com? It helps get the word out to others.
Thanks again!
Rebecca

Acknowledgments

It's been fun to write another Jane Austen retelling. As always, I am so grateful to Jane Austen and her literary legacy. The more I learn about her, the more I am in awe of all she accomplished in her short lifetime.

I also want to express my gratitude for Alfred Hitchcock, as well as the actors and artists who worked with him. It was so fun to bring a little bit of Hitchcock into my writing.

So many people helped bring this book to life. I'd like to thank Renae Mackley, Janice Sperry, and Carolyn Twede Frank, who read and sometimes re-read this story, adding their talents to my creation.

My family, as usual, has been so patient with my writing hobby. My husband Eric helped me brainstorm ideas, watched movies with me, and edited the manuscript. (It's so nice to be married to a professional editor.) Meanwhile, my children only complained a little about the time I spent writing.

Above all, I want to thank my Heavenly Father for supporting me in everything.

ABOUT THE AUTHOR

     Rebecca H. Jamison has lived on a live volcano, excavated the bones of a prehistoric mammal, and won first prize at a rigged chili cook-off. She wrote novels just for fun until she made a New Year's resolution in 2011 to submit a manuscript to publishers.

     Rebecca grew up in Virginia. She attended Brigham Young University, where she earned a BA and MA in English. In between college and graduate school, she served a mission to Portugal and the Cape Verde islands. Her job titles have included special education teacher's aide, technical writer, English teacher, and stay-at-home mom.

     Rebecca enjoys running, dancing, reading, and watching detective shows. She lives with her husband and children in Utah.

     Learn more about her at www.rebeccahjamison.com.

Made in the USA
Lexington, KY
25 October 2019